A challenge sticks in the mind like a litany

– James Cummins

THE NOVELIST

a novella

l . l . b a r k a t

ts T. S. Poetry Press • New York

T. S. Poetry Press
Ossining, New York
Tspoetry.com

This novella includes various references from or to the following brands & sources: *Letters to a Young Novelist,* by Mario Vargas Llosa, Picador, 1997; *Plot & Structure,* by James Scott Bell, Writer's Digest Books, 2004; Yahoo! Inc.; *28 Hotel Rooms,* Directed by Matt Ross, 2012; Lipton Tea brand, Unilever; Twitter Inc.; Aleve brand, Bayer Healthcare, LLC; *The Tale of Genji,* Murasaki Shikibu, translated by Royall Tyler, Penguin Classics, 2006; *The Republic of Tea,* Mel Zeigler and Patricia Ziegler, Crown Business, 1994; *The Things They Carried,* Tim O'Brien, Mariner Books, 2009; Hallmark, Hallmark Cards; *Characters, Emotion & Viewpoint,* Nancy Kress, Writer' Digest Books, 2005; Formica brand, Formica Corporation; Sears Toughskins, Sears, Roebuck & Company; *The Dream of a Common Language,* Adrienne Rich, W. W. Norton & Company, 1993.

Thanks to James Cummins, Claire Burge, and Kelly Sauer for agreeing to be named as the real people they are, while allowing the author to fictionalize their lives for the purposes of this work. All other characters are fictional, though some of their stories are true.

Cover image by Sarah Elwell. knittingthewind.blogspot.com

ISBN 978-0-9845531-9-8

Library of Congress Cataloging-in-Publication Data:
Barkat, L.L.
    [Fiction.]
    The Novelist/L.L. Barkat
    ISBN 978-0-9845531-9-8
    Library of Congress Control Number: 2012947795

for James,
who saw a beginning in the end-words

THE END.

She typed finality across the center of the page and closed the laptop with a snap.

What would it be this morning? She turned to her tea cabinet and opened it quietly. Maybe a green jasmine. She could tweet about it later and make Megan smile. Megan would have tweeted something about a new Earl Grey, and they would share fantasies about each other's kitchens and tea cups. Or did Megan use a mug?

This would explain it. Why she typed, "The End." This lack of attention to detail. Shouldn't she know by now what Megan took her tea in? Hadn't she read a few hundred tweets or more, about English Breakfasts and new green blends, a white tea for afternoon, and a cataloging of how many cups Megan had drunk by 9 pm? She had. Over and again, she had.

But she could not recall Megan's imbibing-receptacle-of-choice. A novelist would remember these things. She would even be willing to research about tea, wouldn't she? To create a believable character based on Megan? An authentic character who knew her basic pekoes from her golden tippys?

Novelists were like that. The real ones, anyway. The ones that Nobel Prize winner Mario Vargas Llosa wrote about in *Letters to a Young Novelist*. Flaubert, Proust, Thomas Wolfe.

She hadn't made it past page 5 in Proust, had gotten hopelessly lost in his detailed descriptions and a vague sense that maybe he was in love with his mother. Really in love. Like maybe he would like to nurse again, but not quite like that. This could be wrong. She could have heard that somewhere and not picked it up by page 5 at all.

And had she even read Wolfe? She couldn't remember that either, beyond what Vargas Llosa quoted, which she had just read on

Monday. Thomas Wolfe likened the life of a writer to being infected by a worm that fed on his insides.

A worm?

It got worse. Vargas Llosa loved this image, had thought of it himself and was simply quoting Wolfe to say, *You see? Being a writer is like having an insatiable parasite inside you.*

Vargas Llosa's worm was a tapeworm, and he had rolled out a few anecdotes about real people with real worms, including a few nineteenth-century ladies who purposely swallowed tapeworms that would eat their insides out, for the sake of social effect—along the lines of impressing the in-crowd with their stunningly slender waistlines.

She hated worms. Her own German grandmother had strung them on fishing lines, turned them loose by the hundreds in her garden, even smashed the "bad" ones between her thumb and middle finger, until their green insides popped out like a bilious pearl.

Laura put her hand to the edge of the granite countertop, feeling suddenly sick. A light sweat broke out across the back of her neck and a warmth spread through her limbs.

She'd better sit down on the floor, right here. Maybe someone would find her dead a few months from now, when her bills went unpaid and the repo guys jimmied the door.

Her laptop was plugged in, though, and the Word file was still open on the desktop—a single page of a novel she had never started, with the words "The End" typed smack in its center. As she sank to the floor, she managed a laugh. "The End." They'd think it was a suicide note, wouldn't they?

And there she'd be, where she was now, finally, thankfully. Cheek to the cool oak floor, having died of a worm.

Someone's life should be at stake. She had read that somewhere. Maybe James Scott Bell, in *Plot & Structure.*

Life and death. High stakes. This was what readers wanted. She was not sure how Marilynne Robinson had won the Pulitzer with a novel about an old man sitting in a placid room, looking out the window day after day, writing letters to his son.

But Marilynne had done it. Won the Pulitzer without an ounce of bloodletting or a single wayward strike of lightning. It could be that the Pulitzer people gave Marilynne points for her previous novel, which apparently had a fire, which was, at least, the death of a house. It was unclear how these prize things worked, but Robinson had won.

Laura turned onto her back and studied the kitchen ceiling. If she lay here long enough, having obviously not died of a worm-induced heart attack, she might yet die of a kitchen ceiling.

The ceiling had not a *worm,* but a long snake. Three of them, in fact, where the water from her shower upstairs had traveled in rivulets and seeped through 1930's plaster, causing the paint to bubble and split and crack—yes, *snake* in ivory-rust patterns.

She had seen a news story on the Yahoo home page, about a hundred-year-old woman in a small village in Italy, who died of a ceiling. Well, technically, it was an earthquake. But the long and short of it was that the woman's bedroom ceiling had collapsed over her big oaken bed, thus bringing to an end a life of wine and pasta and maybe a week of mending (for the house dresses in the closet were in need). So the bright side was—no sewing—but it had come at great sacrifice.

Laura had thought to write a poem about the woman's death-by-ceiling. She did that from time to time: write about tragedies. There'd been the Japan tsunami poem that included a pearl button and a spool of virgin white thread. There'd been the French-Brazilian aircrash-over-the-ocean poem; it was the one with the little boy who was dreaming of *gâteau*. And a poem on Haiti's earthquake, but it almost didn't count, having been focused on an empty tortilla plate.

This was a problem. Her inability to stick with high-stakes subjects, to take her main character and dangle him (or her) over the precipice like F. Scott Fitzgerald promised to do.

"Pull your chair to the edge of the precipice," Fitzgerald had written in one of his many notebooks, "and I will tell you a story." The best novelists were sadistic at heart, able to torture their characters, to hold them at gunpoint for the sake of a good story. The Pulitzer people had forgotten this when awarding Marilynne, but that did not make it any less true.

Laura did not like heights, or precipices, or conflicts. This felt ridiculously problematic. If a writer wasn't going to write for the worm, she should, at the very least, write for the thrill of a good drama, which required high stakes and a precipice or five.

The conflict-avoidance deficit had become clear to Laura, undeniably, when she was with Geoffrey Bloom, her former professor at Yale.

That was wrong. She hadn't actually *gone* to Yale. She'd applied. The "former professor at Yale" designation was simply to say that she was no longer with Geoffrey, thus making him former. And that he was a professor at Yale.

Geoffrey was a comparative literature professor. She had wanted to study comparative literature. The closest she had come to this dream was to date Geoffrey for twenty-eight months. Over two years of her life, and, yes, twenty-eight hotel rooms, she had finally come to understand the truth about herself.

The hotel room arrangement, like something from a strange movie, was a preference of Geoffrey's, who had the means for such luxury. Not that they never went to his house or hers, but that lovemaking was reserved for the once-a-month hotel rooms, where it was a foregone conclusion that they would leave the room and its sheets and let someone else clean up the evidence of what she had, for a long time, wished was love.

It was the twenty-eighth hotel room where the truth had revealed itself, when Geoffrey asked her quite suddenly, "Don't you think life is more interesting when people are against you?" The question had seemed ill put in the golden light, her breasts exposed—a moment when what she really wanted was to feel joined to him and cherished by him.

She had opened her mouth to say "no," but not before he bit her left nipple, too hard to qualify as playfulness, but not hard enough to warrant an accusation of trespass.

The "no" died on her tongue. And she knew in that moment that she was weak. Just the kind of woman who might die of a kitchen ceiling, despite the fact that she did not have the stomach to make a single character—in a novel she had not even started—face death by snake, or plaster, or a lack of love in one too many hotel rooms.

The biggest problem was finding an idea. What to write about?

A woman in her book club worked for Amistad, the publisher of Edward P. Jones's *The Known World*. "He wrote it in three weeks, you know," Beth had announced to the group. Three weeks. Too many characters to count. Overlapping plot lines. A big idea: slavery.

Jones was a two-time National Book Award Finalist. Why hadn't he won the Pulitzer like Marilynne? Laura suspected it was the three-week thing. It might not even be true. Maybe Beth had misheard. Maybe Jones wrote the book in three months.

Did it matter? Respectable books probably took longer. *Faust*, for instance. Sixty years in the making. Jones should have pretended he had struggled for years with that cast of characters. The lightning bolt that had changed his blueberry-picking character's life in a moment should have been reserved for the character alone, not for Jones himself. Nobody likes to think you can be walking along with no idea and the next minute have everything laid out before you like the landscape under a brilliant crack of lightning. Well, Laura would like to think that, was waiting for it, so she could finally start writing. But the Pulitzer people probably reserved their prize for a well-researched novel—pored over, struggled through, ripped up, turned over, begun again. Simplicity was not respectable. A singular idea. One character, or two. Jones had a chance with all those characters and the colorful weaving and reweaving of story lines, but he ruined his chances with the three weeks or three months. It was too simple. He should have known that.

Still, Laura envied Jones. He had accomplished, in some variation of three, a whole National-Book-Award-Finalist novel.

She had "The End" typed across an otherwise blank page. These words didn't even qualify as a poem, unless you were into Saroyan.

People had been into Saroyan for a while. Whole poems like "i crazy" or "coffee coffee" seemed to communicate some kind of infinite and complex message. Either that, or people were tired of T. S. Eliot's long ramblings that required a Ph.D. to understand.

In any case, she was not Saroyan, and this novel she was attempting was not a poem. And, to be honest, even her poems were not prize-winning material, though Geoffrey had claimed to like them. Sometimes she would write him ten poems in a day, and the poems would pile up in his email. Poems like...

Come,
tangle yourself
in me.

Geoffrey had called her his Little Basho, probably because her poems were so short, or maybe because she was always drunk on words, the way Basho had been—little cups of words scattered everywhere, like tea cups or wine glasses piled on an eccentric old woman's sideboard.

Geoffrey said her poems were the sexiest poems he had ever read. *Ever.* And he had read a lot of poems, in languages she would never understand. Japanese, Russian, French, German.

You had to know, or be willing to acquire to a scholarly-level, three languages if you were enrolled in the Yale comparative literature program. At least you had to at the time Laura had applied. She was woefully behind, having only an unimpressive grasp of Spanish and the beginnings of French.

Geoffrey knew five languages fluently and could make his way in countless more. He was a man far beyond Laura's known world, but he liked her poems, or so he said. Still, she had always had a nagging feeling, from the beginning, that she was too provincial for him. Even her word-choices were common. She had ventured a poem about her fear, dropped it in his in-box one midnight when she couldn't stop ruminating about how she'd eventually lose Geoffrey to some woman who could make love to him in Russian, then follow up with small talk in French. The poem was about her mother, but she figured Geoffrey would decode it psychologist-style, and read her between the lines...

Lambent

You see, it is more complicated
than that. I said it was the untutored search
for *lambent, astral, welter,* and the *river of stars.*

But my mother would not know
the meaning of *lambent, welter, astral—*
though the river of stars

is a place she walked me, pointing
on the darkest nights, when I suppose
she wanted to escape her memories

and show me something of the world,
the kind of something only she
could show me.

What did she know of astral predictions,
when she simply walked the nights to forget
the welts of time

and the long-gone days her father's boots

met her mother's face in the lambent
living room, where kerosene lamps

could not light her hiding place
beneath the sideboard (why was the sideboard
in the living room?)

You see the complication now.
And how a passel of big talk
tells her this: what do you know

of the world? You never even learned
to chop an onion, through its many
moistened skins. You couldn't keep

my father, Ivy man of words...
when all you knew was the river,
and the stars.

The stars. These had belonged to her mother, and now they
belonged to Laura. She seemed to remember some character in
Jones's book who looked up at the stars and had an epiphany.
It might not be true. It could have been another book altogether.
But if Jones had made a character look up to the stars, this might
have been his actual problem. This, and the three-variable. It was
too simple to look to the stars; the Greeks and Romans had covered
that territory long ago.

Even so, there were no stars in Laura's kitchen. Just the ceiling
snakes and Vargas Llosa's worms, neither of which she had died
from yet. Maybe she should get off the floor now and make a cup
of tea.

In the end, she had attended New York University. NYU may not have been Yale, but it had a Bloom to its name. Harold, that is.

Laura had refused to take even one class with this famous literary critic. Stories abounded about how Bloom verbally sliced his students and served them up like sushi, to be swallowed in one inelegant bite. The mere thought made her heart beat faster and her fingers tingle. So she never tested the stories for herself, but in this way also avoided the possibility of being drowned in literary-political soy sauce and eaten whole.

Where was the damned tea basket? She pillaged the old wooden drawer, searching for mesh that would keep her loose tea in check. Laura loved loose tea, had developed a taste for it through Geoffrey—a thought that now irritated her. It seemed unfair that he should get the credit for something so important to her life. But it was true. Geoffrey had taught her to love silvery green leaves that curled in on themselves and black leaves that smelled of caramel and brushed against each other like a thousand tiny boats capsized and captured in a fragrant tin.

It was at NYU that she had read Thomas Pynchon, back in the day when she was still a girl who drank Lipton tea. Well, it would be more accurate to say that she had *skimmed* Pynchon's book called *V*, the title of which reminded her simply of a vagina.

This was probably Pynchon's intention, or so it seemed to her now. What she remembered was the lack of a plot in this painfully long book that seemed to be saying, "Life has no plot, why should fiction." The book felt like a grand experiment with a Big Idea, but in fact was terrifically boring. Harold Bloom might find her provincial for thinking this, although she had never read Bloom on Pynchon. Still, if he was like other literary critics, he would love *V*. Literary critics seemed to love stuff like Pynchon's, that somehow avoided looking up at the stars and instead focused on the phallic.

It was all she recalled about the book—some woman who drove a car with a rather endowed stick shift and a group of guys chugging beer in a bar that delivered inebriation from silver kegs to urgent mouths, via huge breast-like feed lines.

Sex could be like death. She understood that. So, technically, Pynchon was on to something, but it was only in a Big Idea way, in her opinion, because there was no one to love in his pages, no one to care for or hope that she (or he) could face whatever death an author would confront the character with, thus presenting a chance for some kind of resilience, even if, at the last, she (or he) died.

Still, writing like Pynchon was an option. Her own life's trajectory bore out his assertion. Nothing really happened. There had been no Door Number One she walked through that led to Door Number Two (was that also James Scott Bell on plot?) that ultimately led to some kind of climax. She could have been one of Pynchon's characters, moving through her days with nothing much to look forward to except Geoffrey's phallus in a hotel room, and even that was no longer a part of her plot line.

Laura spent her days as an advertising copywriter, in a big firm in New York City. She was not comparing Rumi to Basho, but baby wipes to moist cotton clouds. It was a kind of poetry, she had told herself again and again. Plus, it paid the bills far better than her love poems ever could.

This copywriting success was what enabled her to be here, at age forty, in a 1930's Tudor that was perched on the edge of a hill overlooking the age-old Hudson River. Writing baby wipes into the hands of mothers everywhere allowed her to stand here, right here, and desperately rifle through an old wooden drawer, in search of an elusive tea basket.

Megan had been playfully bothering her for a while now. "You should write a novel."

Where Megan had cooked up such a wild idea was beyond Laura. After all, their relationship had been conducted mostly by Twitter, a pastime that was all tea-business for Megan and all pleasurable-escape for Laura. You couldn't know enough about a person through a series of text boxes that held 140 characters or less, to make a judgment like, "You should write a novel." Megan had lost her mind.

Laura closed the wooden drawer with a shove and turned her back to the granite countertop. Leaning back, she tried to mentally retrace the tea basket's possible steps to non-arrival.

Tracing steps, following set paths, was something Laura was both all-too-good-at and not good at in the least. When it came to life, she had more than tried the formulas, attempted to follow the "right" paths. But life had been stacked against her. This was why, she knew, she'd never really had a chance at going to Yale.

Yale was money. And the right clothes. It was your mother knowing how to teach you the secrets of upper-class hair and makeup. It was the string of pearls and the genteel laugh.

But, as Geoffrey had once said, Laura was a gypsy. He said it teasingly, and she had written him a poem about it, complete with palatial reference to a foreign country—maybe to prove she was not really a gypsy or its equivalent… a girl who had somehow broken free of her roots as white trash and was making an impressive living moving words around for baby wipes companies, or the makers of Christmas-tree air fresheners, or even the big drug companies promoting the next Aleve.

The poem was called, not surprisingly, "Gypsy," and it had gone like this…

Don't say
I didn't warn you
about the rosemary;
she will hold it out to you
as you walk past
this little shop to the left,
the one where they are selling
postcards of the Alhambra
at sunset (always at sunset,
when the arches and curves,
and the multi-lingual history
looks best).

Don't say you didn't want it—
the rosemary, and the way
she will look into your palm,
into your tea,
tell you everything
she sees.

Right now, if there was a gypsy in Laura's life, it was not *Laura* at all. It was Megan. Laura had accepted the rosemary from her, so to speak, or maybe the golden tippys, and Megan was looking straight into her heart, with this request for a novel.

It was unsettling. Almost unsettling enough to qualify as Door Number One, if someone had wanted to make a novel of Laura's life.

Door Number One was a neat writing-organization trick that James Scott Bell had discussed in *Plot & Structure*. It was how you were supposed to get from the beginning to the middle of the novel, from Act I to Act II (there being three Acts altogether). Bell had even included a chart and some clip art, to illustrate the concept that, in the end, was quite simple: The main character must be booted through the doorway, into "the great unknown" or the novel would get boring.

Laura thought Bell would have a few things to say to Pynchon. And Laura had a few things to say to Bell, like, How the hell was a writer supposed to know when she was one-fifth through her novel-writing, so she could cut a door into the wall and shove her character out into the forest? It was all too calculated for Laura, like a sonnet with its own version of fifths.

She had tried to work with the sonnet, because it seemed like a poet's badge of honor—a form that would place you shoulder to shoulder with the big boys... Yeats and Keats and Shakespeare. Or was Shakespeare, whose origins were questionable, really a girl? It didn't matter. The world thought Shakespeare was a man, and Laura could not write in his form.

She had tried over and again to conquer the sonnet, even sharing a fun poem called "She" with Geoffrey (in which she, Laura, was both herself and Petrarch's and maybe Geoffrey's, muse). "Leave the sonnets to the big boys," Geoffrey had said. "I prefer my little Basho." Then he had leaned forward and put his hand under her shirt and whispered a date and the name and location of the next hotel. In a fleeting way, this moment had made her feel like a low-class writing whore, but she ignored the pang and made a mental note to add the hotel information to her calendar.

So the problem with Door Number One was, to Laura's mind, a problem of calculation and formula, neither of which she seemed to grasp when it came to a creative process like novel-writing. She wondered vaguely how Mary Shelley had ever got on without Bell, writing her masterpiece by age nineteen. And apparently, others had wondered this too. Not so much about Bell, but about Mary's ability to craft a success so young, and that after her feminist mother had died within ten days of Mary's birth. It shouldn't have been possible, and thus many believed the novel was actually her husband Percy's.

But the novel was hers, and perhaps she had got on without Bell because she had sat around her father's place with, yes, the philosophical big boys, having tea and discussing a whole different set of Big Ideas besides Door Number I and II in three Acts.

Did Mary drink loose tea? And, if so, what had she used to contain it? Maybe Laura would research that sometime, but for today she had a different task at hand—either find the lost tea basket or create a makeshift sifter of leaves.

Laura's mother lived in the country, in upstate New York, where she had lived from the time she was a child, having moved simply the way an old wooden rowboat might move around a back yard pond—drifting from one small town to another, as she had shifted from marriage to marriage.

There had been a time when Laura's mother had begun to make something of herself, and this had seemed important to the small woman who had lost her own mother to long work hours in the textile factory and to days of her father's fists finding release on her mother's body. The effect of these losses could not be calculated, except perhaps in the stories Laura's mother told. Stories of goldenrods and flies and mischievous projects undertaken in the living room by her and her siblings.

Laura had cried over the goldenrod story, as she had cried over so many of her mother's simple stories. She wondered if this response made *her* simple, or if it was merely a testament to the power of her mother's ability with the briefest of narratives.

"On the way to school one day, I picked goldenrods for my 1st-grade teacher, Mrs. Jordan. I added some timothy for extra green and fixed them up nice together." Here, her mother had always paused in the story, to let Laura get a hold on the images and the situation, to let her enter the story as if she herself was the child with goldenrods now in her hand.

"It was the most beautiful bouquet! And I knew it would make Mrs. Jordan very happy."

In the kitchen, the tea basket's disappearance escaping Laura's consciousness for the moment, she closed her eyes, picturing the rest of the scene. Her mother's almond eyes, beaming. Her mother's tiny milk-white hands reaching up to the teacher. And the simultaneous snap of the teacher's voice and hand, "Those are weeds, Cora Martin. Throw them in here." Mrs. Jordan had swooped up the grey rubber trashcan and shoved it into Cora's space. "Throw them in. Right now. That's it. We can't have weeds in the classroom."

And Laura's mother had done it. Had dropped the common golden field flowers in with crumpled papers and pencil filings and somebody's bloody hanky, which had to be tossed because of a nosebleed.

The loss of Cora's childhood seemed to gather and concentrate in this story. The child, the search for beauty, the offer, the tossing. Laura never tired of the story, and her mother had told it many times over the years.

Her mother's eight-grade math teacher had his own place in the hall of stories, having called Cora *stupid* when she couldn't calculate at the blackboard and having remarked, on the first day of class, "Oh, you're a Martin? They're around here like flies."

So it seemed important when her mother finally made it through school, graduated and went on to do light accounting and reception work at Albany Medical Center, one of the best hospitals in the region, where Cora got to wear a crisp white nurse's outfit (though she wasn't a nurse) and thick-heeled white shoes that made her taller and propelled her with a measure of confidence over the bleached and waxed floors.

It was probably this newfound confidence, or the shortness of Cora's skirt, that attracted Laura's father. That, or the almond eyes, set above high cheekbones and framed by a trim cut of sassy black hair.

When Laura first met Geoffrey, she had tried to explain what happened next, in the narrative of a poem. It only explained origins, of course, but it contained the seeds of endings too...

What's that?
I say, and turn to see you watching me.

Go back, you whisper, coming close,
lifting my hem a little higher.

Okay...

They were young.
She was French and Indian (through Canada),
but they say she looked like Cleopatra.

It was night,
and she and he drove closer to the stars,
somewhere in the Helderbergs

(there is a castle in those hills, I hear,
built by a philosopher, potter, poet).

The sky, I think, was black and red,
too much, as it were, and then
he raised her hem—

for the universe knew, it knew:
you would have need of me.

In order for the universe to receive the privilege of Laura, her mother had to quit her job at Albany Med and make things right by marrying Laura's father. So it was the first and last professional job her mother ever held; the conception of Laura permanently changed her mother's trajectory.

It was in this altered life state—her mother working for a local McDonald's—that Geoffrey had met Cora, her sassy black hair long gone and her milk-white skin replaced by a reddish complexion obtained from hours of planting flowers or picking up trash in the store's parking lot.

Cora had told Geoffrey her Indian-in-the-forest story, over a blue-rose cup of Lipton tea, in the kitchen of her trailer, the windows of which were hung with cream lace curtains and amethyst crystals she had collected and restrung from a necklace she'd found at a garage sale.

The Indian was probably not an Indian, but Cora had encountered him, as he peered through the branches, while she walked the lines of an old property owned by a friend who wanted ideas for a vintage garden.

Long black hair and war paint on his cheeks, the Indian had pulled down a branch, ever so slowly, to get a look at Laura's mother, who, when she saw his coal-black eyes, had turned her body and walked like a woman lightning-struck and shaking, back to her friend's house, where she made excuses and then left and neglected to ever return for the planning of the garden.

On the long drive back to Connecticut, Geoffrey remarked that, for a woman of such narrow surroundings, Cora certainly had a wide imagination. It didn't surprise him that Laura had turned to poetry as a form of structured consolation and a subtle way to raise herself above such quaint roots, even if Laura wasn't writing sonnets. Then he reached across the shift of the Volvo and placed his hand softly on Laura's knee, reciting in a resonant and soothing voice, "Let me not to the marriage of true minds admit impediments. Love is not love which alters when it alteration finds…" His hand on her knee, and the words of love recited: This got Laura every time. Geoffrey had a deep talent for overcoming her.

Megan had over 100,000 followers on Twitter, which was why Wednesday night had been a total cliff-edge, at least to Laura.

Laura's own audience was nothing much. About three hundred followers, many of whom she mostly ignored. Except for Megan. Megan had a way of delighting Laura with tweets about her daily tea habits and her burgeoning business.

On Wednesday, around 8 pm, Laura had tweeted to Megan, "I want your new Bagatelle."

"One Bagatelle, and I'll raise you a novel," Megan had tweeted back.

"Writing for tea? Now that would have been a solution for the British empire," Laura returned.

"Writing for me," Megan had typed.

"I'll write you a tea fortune."

"No deal. I want a novel. September sounds good."

Megan had added the hashtag #amwriting to her final challenge tweet, and a good number of the writing audience that paid attention to that sort of thing had retweeted the challenge. After that, Laura had to lie down, she'd felt so weak in the knees.

The thing about Megan was, you couldn't say no to her. This was how she'd been building her tea empire, one contact at a time, a truckload of tweets a week, and with trips to India and China.

So Laura had come to the blank screen today, if only to assuage Megan with, "I tried." After which, she hoped Megan would drop the matter, and Laura could go back to entertaining Megan with her catchy copywriting-style tweets about simple things like tea baskets and the alternative uses for Lipton tea bags.

Tea baskets. Where the hell had hers gone off to? The house was only 800 square feet. More like a cottage really. Geoffrey always said it was the perfect size for his Little Basho, a remark which secretly irritated her, because what she wished she had—not to be ungrateful—was a house with a small sitting room and a window seat where she could create trails of treasures like the pearly orange-cupped seashells she had found when they went to Long Island one weekend.

She consoled herself with gathering such treasures into poems instead...

> At the end of the Sound,
> where the pines have been pushed back
> by an unrelenting salt wind,
> you will find that jingle-shell beach—
> where little cups of pearly lemon peach
> stretch out endlessly. Put your hands to them
> and you will not know
> where to stop.
>
> So much beauty,
> so much unrelenting jingle-chiming
>
> beauty.

She had mentioned once, to Geoffrey, her desire for the treasure room with its pearly peach seashells, and he broke out in an uncharacteristically loud laugh, "You've got a whole house to yourself, Laura! What do you need with a room for souvenirs and kitsch?" She had gone quiet then, and he apologized for laughing, saying she was a quirky little poet after all, and this was probably what made her so prolific. People without quirks had less to write about. That was his theory.

If Laura was so prolific with poems, and in truth she was, then what was the problem with Megan's request? Couldn't Laura, with a little doing, keep stringing together line after line of words and construct, in time, a novel? It seemed logical, but there was the matter of finding an idea and sustaining it. Only fire could do that. *The fire of rebellion.*

Mario Vargas Llosa had not used the term "fire" exactly, but rather had discussed the presence of "seditious roots" that could "dynamite the world" the writer inhabited. He claimed that writing stories was an exercise in freedom and quarreling—out-and-out rebellion, whether or not the writer was conscious of it. And this rebellion, Vargas Llosa reminded his readers, was why the Spanish Inquisition had strictly censored works of fiction, prohibiting them for three hundred years in the American colonies.

Laura suddenly longed for an Inquisition-style prohibition, to magically step between her and Megan. But she had the feeling that not even a major historical movement could rescue her from this threat.

Opening the tea cabinet again, Laura began shifting teas around, as if she might organize a rebellion by reorganizing the position of the greens in relation to the blacks.

This was ridiculous, completely ridiculous. Laura had nothing to rebel about. She had not a single idea for a novel, nor the ability to sustain one if she found it. This was too hard, and Megan had been wrong to humiliate her. Not that the people on Twitter really knew who @LauraSilva was. But Laura knew who she was.

Or maybe she didn't.

Ridiculous. This thing with Megan was ridiculous. She slammed the tea cabinet shut, grabbed her red sneakers, and walked out of the house. It was raining.

Beyond the door, under the small porch roof, with its ivory wainscot ceiling, Laura had placed a rickety card table she'd picked up
from the side of the street. Where she lived, people often placed
their bulk trash out a few days early, to accommodate the multi-
tudinous classes of trash pickers—from students who might need
free dorm-room décor, to construction workers and trash resellers,
to the poor who might be searching for a new (old) couch. Laura
had spotted the card table and carted it home.

She pulled aside a wooden folding chair and sat down near the
table, placing the sneakers on the blue cotton tablecloth. Laura
loved these red sneakers. They matched almost nothing she
owned, but she loved them, and now she began playing with the
laces, tying and untying them with an artful movement, as if test-
ing their best existential condition.

The rain was *tip, tip, tipping,* and she began to mull to its
rhythm. In retrospect, she thought, it had probably been a mistake to begin her relationship with Geoffrey via a sestina. Sestinas
were complex, or they could be, poems of thirty-nine lines, with
repeating end words that shifted places in a rolling fashion, until
they ended up belly to belly, shoulder to back, in the final three
lines of the poem.

Her sestina, after all, had been an outlier—a response to a
challenge from her friend James Cummins, a poet she had met at
a reading and followed up with by email. James had the heart of
a teacher (and a mischief-maker) and had somehow perhaps seen
possibility in Laura. One day, she found this challenge from him,
daring her in the in-box, "Write a sestina using the following teleu-
tons: Delft, tea caddy, Betjeman and Barton, rosewood, avoirdupois, porcelain." Then he'd added, "If somebody gave me this
challenge, I'd find a way to avoid it."

Laura looked at the end words he proposed, and she laughed. James wasn't kidding. This was an impossible task. *Avoirdupois?* Damn. She didn't even know what that was. Nor *Delft*. *Tea caddy* was right up her alley and the purveyor *Betjeman and Barton* was dear to her loose-tea-loving heart.

"I'm working on a big project, James. Due in a week. Maybe I'll get to your challenge after that and after I figure out the nature of *avoirdupois* and Delft," she'd responded. But then the challenge from James, like Vargas Llosa's worm, wiggled its way into her psyche. She was distracted from her work project and felt she could not rest until she took up the challenge. So that was it. Two hours later, after researching each end-word online, then turning it this way and that on paper, she sent James this sestina:

The Proposal

"Perhaps, let's go to Delft,"
he said, taking the silver tea caddy
gingerly off the shelf. It was Betjeman and Barton—
not the shelf, which was of rosewood,
but the caddy painted slight with numbers, *avoirdupois,*
the weight of tea I steep to pour in porcelain.

"Why should we?" I lifted porcelain.
Not the kind they make in Delft—
copied from the Chinese, high-resistance, unlike the
measure *avoirdupois*
adopted through a confluence of words...Latin, French
as the tea caddy
I opened for the promise, that petaled-rose would
spread its fragrance with Darjeeling; Betjeman and
Barton

sell it so. I wonder if it's Betjeman or Barton
who dreamed of almonds, grapes and peonies to drift in
    porcelain.
Who bare-suggested in a whisper that a hint of rose
    would
be a better choice than, let's just say, a tulip, yellow,
    plucked from Delft?
I mused on Netherland's canals and stretched towards
    the tea caddy.
What if he could weigh my thoughts in dark *avoirdupois*?

A measure partly from the Latin, *avoirdupois*
came over from *to have, to hold, possess,* like the
    Betjeman and Barton
I hold this very moment, twisting cover of a tight-sealed
    tea caddy
which, had it come from long ago, might rather be of
    bone-ash porcelain
hand-painted blue with scenes of domesticity from
    Delft.
Milk maids, windmills, a tulip—not a rose—would

play across it like the Madagascar sun on rosewood
stolen from the tropics, shipped through China,
    measured in *avoirdupois*—
all multiples of which are based on pounds, like stones
    of city walls in Delft.
You cannot find this in the catalog from Betjeman
    and Barton,
the knowledge that the British added stones as hard as
    fired porcelain,
or that the city once exploded like the fragrance from

this silver tea caddy,

assaulting air and narrow streets with powder they don't
   sell in tea caddies,
brass-mounted, inlaid carefully, satin-wood or rosewood,
the larger ones called tea chests, often seated near the
   porcelain
in dining rooms where merchandise bears not the paint
   of bold *avoirdupois*
but is quite fragrant with rare teas of fine purveyors.
   Betjeman and Barton
is my favorite, see, residing in the heart of passion—
   Paris—not in Delft.

I place the silver tea caddy directly on the shelf,
   unpainted with the weight of ebony *avoirdupois*,
silver tipped with fresh-spilled leaves scattered on the
   rosewood, lined with Betjeman and Barton
rarities to pour into my porcelain, which would, I tell
   him, *never* come from Delft.

James was delightfully surprised, despite some of the technical
frailties of the sestina. He spent the next few days helping her understand the nuances of something as simple as a comma versus
a period, which, in a poem, can provide for a marked increase in
tension or a subtle change in pacing. In the end, James had liked
the poem enough to publish it on *The Best American Poetry* blog,
complete with the story of its advent, and a fine compliment about
how Henry James himself might have written such a poem, had he
written sestinas.

   It was this sestina she'd sent to Geoffrey on a whim, about
three emails into a correspondence she'd struck up with him to

deliver a compliment about a piece he'd written for The Poetry Foundation. Geoffrey had asked if she wrote poetry and she'd said, why yes, and sent along "The Proposal."

"My, what a big sestina you have, my dear," he'd teased her in response, but then made a proposal of his own: Come to New York City, would she? He was going to be there next month, for an evening of discussion of medieval poetry in Japan and China.

She put on a sassy black suit, and came.

It was a light rain, and Laura decided to step into it. She put the red sneakers on—first the left, and then the right, lacing each one tightly as if trying to contain herself.

Geoffrey disliked rain, said he had a cat instinct, a kind of retracting impulse when the droplets touched his face. Laura had observed this on the night they met, and it made her laugh.

"Afraid you'll melt?" she'd asked.

And he'd remarked about the cat instinct and offered her his shelter under a large black umbrella. She took cover, leaning in close, as they walked to the Princeton Club, where Geoffrey was staying. Would she like some tea, he'd asked, after the poetry lecture. The Princeton would have it, and they could sit in the library and continue talking poetry if she liked.

She liked. And so they walked beneath the black umbrella until they reached the great brassy double doors of the club and stepped into the dry air.

"Mr. Bloom," a concierge nodded as they entered, and Geoffrey had returned the greeting with a "good evening."

As it turned out, she and Geoffrey never got the tea, nor did they sit in the staid old library. She was carrying a large leather bag, already overstuffed, and had filled it further by purchasing a few books at the lecture, including a two-inch thick anthology of Chinese poetry, for which Geoffrey had served as editor, and a volume of *The Tale of Genji*.

"Looks like a heavy bag," he'd said, and offered to stash it in his room upstairs, while they went searching for tea. He had said it casually, as if he'd said it a hundred times before and no longer needed practice. Laura noticed this as if without noticing, then she understood the offer for what it was and realized she might, after all, miss out on tea in favor of intimate company. She took the chance.

"Ah, Murasaki," he had whispered and kissed her bare shoulder, after removing her black wool suit to reveal a plum-colored camisole. Then he'd undone her, strap by strap, layer by layer, until he had come to her breasts and taken them, one after the other, into his smooth hands, then onto his tongue. It had been forever, she thought, since someone had made her feel so beautiful. The closeness overcame her.

When she returned home on the train, late that night, she had sent him a poem to remember the moment…

The Tale of Genji: Abridged, by

Murasaki
was not her real name.

*

Did you know that *Murasaki*
means purple?

*

When they bound up Genji's boyish hair,
the cord they used was

*

Did you know (how could you?)
that the first time a reader chose to insult my work,
    she called it

*

Purple is the color of closeness.
The cord was

*

Murasaki
is her real name.

Murasaki had been born in 973, to a minor branch of an otherwise powerful family. Her name had gone unrecorded, being that she was only a daughter. But the nickname, *Murasaki,* had survived along with what was now recognized as a major masterpiece of fiction—ranking as high in Japan as the Homeric epics, Shakespeare's works, and Proust's *Remembrance of Things Past.* Murasaki had probably come to serve the empress Akiko because of her talent for writing fiction. That was the theory.

Geoffrey had explained a good deal of this in his lecture, remarking on the irony that though fiction was below the dignity of Japanese men of the time, it was men who ultimately championed the complex work which also contained (more to their liking) 795 poems. Poetry being considered the noblest of arts, it was perhaps also ironic that the "best poet" in the *Tale* was the Akashi lady. But perhaps this was not irony after all, Laura had thought later, considering that Murasaki may have purposely, rebelliously put the best poetic words in Akashi's mouth—the mouth of a woman.

If Murasaki could write a work of fiction, in an environment that didn't respect it, why couldn't Laura set down at least one paragraph, to entertain a friend who was asking her for a story? It was a good question. But, so far, she didn't have a good answer as to why she could only eke out "The End."

Laura stepped out from under the wainscot ceiling and let the rain play against her upturned hands. She wondered idly if Megan liked rain and thought to perhaps tweet the question, if she could find a way to do it that didn't seem too oddly personal. But she was also nervous that if she tweeted again anytime soon, Megan might bring up the novel. Perhaps it was best to make herself scarce for a while. What if she just happened to get lost outside, walking around in the rain or camping out under the big old pine tree at the back of the yard? Maybe no one would notice her absence, least of all Megan with her crazy dreams.

10

"You have a flair for the narrative in your poems, Laura. I think you can do this."

In desperation, she'd decided to contact James and tell him her novel-sob-story. She sat now on the porch, having gone back in briefly to grab her laptop so she could start a chat with James.

"It's pathetic, James. I've been wandering around my back yard all afternoon, like Little Red Riding Hood without my basket (did I tell you I lost my tea basket?). And it's all because somebody challenged me to write a novel, and I can't get past the words, 'The End.'"

James typed a smiley face. "Well, that's as good a place as any to start," he said. "A writer can't be fussy. You haven't gone all fussy on me, have you, Laura? Are you sure you aren't the Princess and the frog? Little Red wasn't fussy, the way I see it. Start anywhere. Write anything. Like that Barkat woman says, 'Just begin.'"

He was referencing a simple poem Laura had found and sent him, from a collection by L.L. Barkat...

> Find a single
> tree, find
> the moon.
> It doesn't
> take much.
> Just begin.

"It's not the beginning I'm so worried about," she told him. "It's the middle. You know, after Door Number One. The great unknown of Act II, where the character has to wander around digging deep into herself, finding courage, learning, making new allies. Damn that James Scott Bell. He makes it sound so easy."

She was not being quite fair. Though Bell did make it sound easy, he also called the middle the "muddle," as if he himself had lived the complication of trying to keep the story alive through the doldrums between the Doors.

Fairy tale writers had reduced this discomforting task greatly, by producing in short form. Little Red could walk into a forest and everyone knew, metaphorically, that she was in the muddle stage. It didn't take long to come to the other side and walk through Door Number Two, conquer the wolf and go her way, *happily ever after*. Laura said as much to James, complaining about Bell, the Grimms, and Miss Red, all in one fell swoop.

But James was resolute. "I see your talent for narrative in the miniature. You just have to open it out."

Mary Shelley had begun *Frankenstein* in the miniature. On a proverbial dark and stormy night, at Lord Byron's place near Lake Geneva, Byron had challenged his guests to a competition: Write a ghost story (and may the best man win). Mary had done it, drawing conveniently on a dream. The end of the competition turned out to be the beginning for Mary, as she later worked the story into a whole book. Taking what had begun as a dare, she made it through the muddle, only to produce an enduring classic.

What made a story endure? Laura typed the question into a brand-new Word file. The cursor sat blinking after the question mark, as if to emphasize the evasive nature of the inquiry.

Thomas Pynchon would not endure, thought Laura, except as a curiosity along the way. The strong stories, the true ever-after stories had plots. The characters could even be somewhat flimsy. Cinderella, Sleeping Beauty: These were not well-developed characters, but cultures across the world all had their versions.

Laura had once bought her niece an entire collection of Cinderella stories, no two exactly the same, yet all containing a similar thread: Poor girl is mistreated and unappreciated. She suffers loss. Hope is kindled through invitation. A helpful guide or magical creature appears. Poor girl overcomes and turns beautiful (which she has been all along), and she is bestowed with attention or riches. It was a tried-and-true formula which storytellers had co-opted for generations, adding numerous twists and sometimes creating anti-stories.

Maybe Laura's real problem came in admitting this: there was nothing new under the sun. To write a story would be, somehow deep down, to embrace her limits, to admit that, indeed, she would someday die—if not of a worm or a ceiling, then of something else. The very nature of a story admitted this reality. To be a writer was to say, yes, I am just another Murasaki, and it is quite possible that no one will remember my name.

"I think I'm afraid to die," she wrote to James after that.

"Of course you are, Laura," he had tenderly returned. "We are all afraid to die."

11

Vargas Llosa said the "curious ambiguity of fiction" was its aspiration to independence, in the midst of an inevitable slavery to reality. Laura liked this idea, though she thought the assertion seemed larger than fiction.

How had Megan done it? Become independent, in a very true sense, despite that she had bills to pay, like everyone else and, like everyone else, was a slave to the reality that someday the bill-paying would end? How had she suspended her fears, if she even had them, and chosen to live into life itself, as if she was an unbelievable storybook character come into the flesh?

Megan Robins tea, Laura typed into the Google search bar. A series of links appeared. *Tea for Two* sat in the top search slot. That was Megan's business name. Images of *Tea for Two* teapots and loose teas tempted Laura to go back into the house and make that lost cup of morning tea. But she stayed on the porch and clicked through to a major bookseller link: *How the Empress Came to Tea, Megan Robins with Sophia Akhmatova.*

Sophia was Megan's partner. They had met on a high-speed train from New York to Boston, when Sophia had boldly inquired about the book Megan held between them: *Tea the Drink that Changed the World.* Laura read about this life-altering encounter in the bookseller's blurb, along with the promise that *How the Empress Came to Tea* would tell the story of how Megan and Sophia hooked up beyond a simple train ride, to become a burgeoning force in the tea business.

The light in Laura's back yard had taken on a golden tone now, and she paused to look up at the wildness blooming near the fringes of her yard. The birds had probably done it—brought the seeds of purple spike flowers, daisies, and those little yellow blossoms that looked like banana boats (this is what Laura and her sister had called these flowers as children, and though Laura was sure they had some proper Latin name, she was tickled by the idea of letting them keep their storied name: banana boats).

Along the wildflower fields, it was Laura's sister who had always done the climbing. Up a displaced apple tree (what was it doing on their property, not part of any orchard or deliberate planting?), up the white pines that towered in various treelines bordering field after field. And Laura had stood at the bottom of the trees, looking up.

Sometimes the sisters chatted that way—Laura at the base, Sherrie gazing over their known world, with glimpses of what lay beyond. It was during those dreamy times that they plotted to run away to their grandmother's house, Sherrie full of confidence that they could pull it off with a few good supplies: matches, peanut butter sandwiches, a map, and a nice brisk walk. Yes, it might take them days and days to accomplish this impossible task of transition, but it could be done.

Laura smiled now to think of it. Why, she had done it, hadn't she? Eventually? She'd left their rural roots and moved to the New York metro area, first as a college student and then for a time actually living with her grandmother while she looked for her first job and apartment. Is that how life worked? Could the impossible really be wrought, with time and unfolding, if a dream was planted deep within?

Maybe there *was* hope for Laura, after all. Though she wasn't quite sure what she was hoping *for,* beyond a cup of tea and at least one page of a novel she could use to appease a persistent friend.

How had Megan done it, Laura wondered again. Well, there was one way to try to find out. Laura clicked the *Download to E-Reader Now* button and paid the $9.99 that must surely be her golden key.

Congratulations! You've just purchased How the Empress Came to Tea. Share your purchase? The bookseller's message popped up after Laura completed her transaction, and she hovered over the Twitter icon.

"Oh, what the hell," she thought. And tweeted her golden key to the world.

12

Megan Willow (@meganwillow) retweeted one of your tweets!
The email alert appeared almost instantaneously. Megan didn't miss a beat, did she. It was like she was some kind of mind reader.

Worse, Megan tweeted back to Laura, "You've got my story, now I want yours! #amwriting #novel"

"Have tea, might write," Laura returned.

"Deal," tweeted Megan.

What did that mean? A sinking feeling spread through Laura's middle. Megan was known for deal making, had been named a Top 10 Woman Entrepreneur by *Forbes* last year. If she could exact the best-priced exotic teas from China, she was quite capable of compelling Laura to write a novel, if only Laura could write it.

Direct message from Meganwillow. The alert popped into her inbox. "Neruda Black Cherry Tea for Two, coming right up. Need your address."

Laura's fingers started tingling. This was a dangerous moment, like taking rosemary from a gypsy. How did she get herself into these things?

"Wandering in the great forest of my yard. Location currently unknown," Laura messaged back.

"Bullshit. Send me your address. We made a deal."

We did? thought Laura. When exactly had that happened?

Mario Vargas Llosa said that the narrator—the person telling the story—shouldn't be confused with the author, and that many novelists made this mistake. They'd take their own biographies, tell the story in first person, and thus believe they were the narrators of their fictions.

Couldn't the same mistake be made when telling the story in third person? Laura believed it could. More than that, she believed this could happen in life. A person could think she was telling her own story, so to speak, only to discover that another narrator had taken the wheel.

It had gone this way with Geoffrey, over time, hadn't it. But who was she kidding. It had gone this way from the beginning, when he offered to stash her bag in his room, and she had let him lead her upstairs into 28 months of what-happened-next. She had played her character well, following him not just the first night, into the first hotel, but into 27 more hotels, each one bringing her further to her knees. Some nights, she felt as if she'd been leveled and chained, and an image of herself face to the floor, hands cuffed, would drift through her mind, along with a fleeting hope that the relationship would end.

Yet she had stayed. Had wanted him more than anything in the world. Until the end, she'd given him the power of narration.

Laura thought back to her mother's mother. Not the grandmother of the runaway-hopes she'd cultivated with her sister. But the grandmother who'd endured kicks and fists and fractures and bruises.

Her grandmother revealed a secret story, once, in a scene that had shocked Laura. She'd told the tale to save Laura's cousin, who'd gotten herself into an abusive relationship and had the bruises to prove it.

"I stayed for the sex," her grandmother had said. And Laura had believed it at the time, though now she felt it was probably not that simple.

"That was a sweet little death," Geoffrey had remarked on their first night together. She'd tilted her head and her eyes must have registered confusion, so Geoffrey had launched into an explanation of the French, *la petite mort*.

It was a term not without its own confusions. On the one hand, it was simply a metaphor for orgasm, though this was based on a deeper possible experience of spiritual release—a sense of either melancholy or transcendence resulting from expenditure of one's "life force." Literary critic Roland Barthes, explained Geoffrey, actually spoke of *la petite mort* as the prime objective of reading literature. But then there was the dark meaning captured by Thomas Hardy's character Tess, when she used the term to describe how it felt to meet her own rapist. In this case, the term meant a person felt she'd somehow died inside.

"But our little death was sweet, Murasaki," Geoffrey had said.

Laura thought now how fine the line could be, between life and death, between handing yourself to one narrator versus another. It didn't seem possible to extricate oneself from this process altogether. People functioned like narrators and characters, one to another. The key was perhaps in the choices a person made, of who to whom.

"12 Marquez Lane, Tarrytown, NY 10591"

Laura typed her address in Megan's reply-to-message box, and hit *Send.*

13

Tea would be on its way. Megan would be sure to send it. Laura knew she could trust that. She also knew bits and pieces of Megan and Sophia's story, since she followed *Tea for Two* and Megan on Twitter. But the pieces seemed as Vargas Llosa said they were, when speaking of an author's life condensed into novel form. "The author has a much richer and fuller life, which predates the novel and survives it."

If this was true for the author and the novel, how much more for a woman and her Twitter stream. Fragments had a way of building up, yes, but it was hard to keep track, and surely a life couldn't be contained in disparate boxes of 140 characters. There would be more to the story, and Laura intended to open up Megan's by reading *How the Empress Came to Tea*.

She went back into the house and grabbed her e-reader and a banana muffin off the counter. Why were her hands shaking? It was just a book about two women meeting for the business of tea.

Laura fumbled with the porch light switch, missed it once and had to begin again. There. Turned on and ready for an evening of reading. She stepped back onto the porch, sat, and rested her e-reader against the edge of the card table. *Open, push button, miracle.* In a minute, she would be holding Megan's story in her hands.

"I found tea at the scene of an accident," said the opening line. The book was written from Megan's perspective. Laura quickly read on. Megan was apparently a tall woman, and strong. She'd met Sophia on the train, but nothing much had come of it. At least not business-wise. They had discerned a shared love of tea, had kept up a correspondence, had even fantasized about a tea enterprise together, but Megan's direction was already set. She was a major player at a big accounting firm. They depended on her expertise, her productivity, her ability to spin anything in any direction. The work was eating Megan alive, though she wasn't conscious of it.

Then one day, she was driving from Boston to Tanglewood, when everything had changed. The car in front of her blew a tire and careened. She slowed to prevent herself from ending up in its path and was successful. But the veering car ran off the road and hit a utility pole. The vehicle burst into flames.

Megan stopped short and rushed from her car, her tall frame approaching what turned out to be a tiny woman sitting in shock in a crumpled vehicle. With the flames leaping and smoke billowing, Megan hardly thought about what she did next—pull the woman from the car to bring her to safety. But the woman was truly in shock and not thinking straight. She rushed onto the highway, into oncoming traffic. Megan acted fast, carrying her back to the shoulder, then pinning her down until another car stopped and called 911, the police arrived, and everything was defused.

It was the flames and the smoke that woke Megan, then and there. She would call Sophia when she got home and begin to make their tea dreams a reality. She would not work a minute longer than she had to at the job that had been sucking the life out of her. Time was too short. The flames and the smoke said that loud and clear.

So Megan's little death had saved her from a different little death. Flames and smoke had taken her to tea. It was a dramatic story, aptly suited to Megan, who seemed to do everything in a big way.

Laura paused. What was it Tim O'Brien had said about stories, in his book *The Things They Carried*? Something about how stories had the power to make things present, how they made it possible for a person to look at things never looked at. It was about being *made brave* and finding you had the ability to feel again.

Twenty-eight months of life with Geoffrey had done the opposite. As much as he loved her poetry, which he did, the over-all effect of their life story together was that it did not make Laura brave. Over time, she felt more and more anxiety about her ability to keep him, and she'd eclipsed a good deal of her personal story to feed the part of him that seemed likely to keep her. If she'd written of something like tea, which she sometimes had, it came out like this...

> Remind me, would you,
> to buy more of the Peach Momotaro,
> with its images of waterfalls, lichen-toned
> terraces, waves of mountains imprinted
> with dots, little white flowers, and mist.
> When I drink it, and the steam enters me,
> I think of you and the water feels as if
> it's pouring over the mountains.

Geoffrey liked this poem. For the Asian influence, the lyricism, the sensuality. But, mostly, for the way it put him in the center of her longing. He hadn't been shy about saying so. Understanding the effect of her words, all her poems eventually became about Geoffrey and sensuality. It was the one place she felt a sense of power. But the power was mostly confined to lines and stanzas and a narrow theme. *Where had Laura gone?*

She closed her eyes for a moment and pictured Megan, as best she could, not ever having seen her in person. She pictured a woman who had maybe asked the same kind of question, at the scene of an accident: *Where have I gone?* Then Megan had set about to bring herself back to life, to be brave and feel again.

What was Laura waiting for? Was it going to take a car wreck, smoke and flames, to stage her rebellion into life? Or could a quieter coup be arranged.

14

Laura switched off *How the Empress Came to Tea* and turned to her laptop. Would James still be on? She started a chat.

"I still haven't written my novel," she typed. "But I've eaten one banana muffin, been bitten by two mosquitoes, and read three chapters of a very inspiring book."

"What book?"

Laura brightened. She really wanted this time with James, though she couldn't explain why. James was old enough to be her father but often treated her like a sweet lover. Chatting with James was a little like dancing in rain. She always felt good being in his presence.

"Would we play like this if we were in person?" he'd asked once. And she sensed the question meant more than what it seemed on the surface. It wasn't simply play. It was a kind of love that could play. And so it was more of a thing and less of a thing. To express it this way made no sense, yet it made perfect sense to Laura. Something like the way Tim O'Brien expressed his thoughts about story-truth. He had a part in his book, so poignant, where he recounted a moment with his daughter...

> "Daddy, tell the truth," Kathleen can say, "did you ever kill anybody?" And I can say, honestly, "Of course not." Or I can say honestly, "Yes."

So Laura could look at James and see how he could be both a lover and not a lover, a father and not a father. Story-truth would allow such variation.

Could life-truth allow it too?

When her father had taken her mother high into those mountains, to conceive her, only later to leave her, could it be understood the way one understands story-truth? Could it have been both a terrible mistake and a gift to the universe?

As a child, Laura could only see it a single way: big mistake. Watching her mother struggle through life as a single mom, then later in a marriage to a violent man, then single, then married, Laura could only trace the line in one direction. Her father should never have done what he did.

On the other hand, her mother had seemed only to be a helpless victim, a young woman taken with the smooth words of a handsome player. Could there be a second, equally-true truth? Story-truth would allow it.

A light breeze picked up, and Laura took to watching the moths circle the porch light, court their death. It was Laura's mother who had, despite everything, introduced her to courage—the kind that could stand its ground in a moment that courted threat. She had done it morning after morning, by reading poetry to Laura and Sherrie, while they sat in the house of a violent man and waited for the school bus to bring another day's reprieve. Laura's mother had chosen wisely, sharing narrative poems like "Charlottie," that warned of the perils of being vain for the sake of a man. And she had included one about a person who had shut out love, in a harsh way. The poem ended...

> But Love and I had the wit to win,
> We drew a circle that took him in.

To Laura, the poem seemed to be about how we don't need to be victims in the face of another person's unkindness. The poem held its share of courage.

But the single event of bravery that stood out in Laura's mind was an incident with a large German shepherd. It had somehow gotten loose and was roaming the neighborhood just when Laura's mother had taken her and Sherrie out for their evening walk. German shepherds are sometimes trained to be fierce guard dogs, and this one must have been. What it was guarding was never clear to the three of them, as they came to the edge of the tree line and it stepped into their path, barking and baring its yellow teeth.

"Stand still," said Laura's mother. She had instinctively put her arms around Laura and Sherrie, and the three of them faced the dog as one. "Stand straight, like you don't intend to be moved. Dogs sense fear. Don't be afraid."

Laura *was* afraid. Her heart raced and her palms began to sweat. But she pretended otherwise to the dog. She and her mother and sister stared the dog down until it gave up barking and baring its teeth and walked back into the woods, disappearing into the shadows, as if it had never come.

But it had come. And Laura thought now how her mother was beautifully strong. This was the truth.

"What book?" The words of James still went unanswered on her screen.

"*How the Empress Came to Tea.*"

"By boat?" James typed, and added a smiley face.

"By accident, like maybe the way I'll write my novel if I ever get to it."

James ignored her smart-aleck comment and went straight to the heart, as she realized he so often did. "Do you want to? Write it, I mean?"

"Yes," she typed.

"And no."

Both answers were true.

15

Megan had set an impossible task before Laura, and Laura wasn't sure what had possessed her to do so. Didn't Megan have enough to attend to, without demanding a novel from someone who'd never even finished a short story? Tea deals and cool catalogs and business trips should have helped Laura escape Megan's notice, but they hadn't.

And now that Laura had Megan's attention, she wasn't sure why she felt compelled to achieve the task. Most things in life that we feel are so beyond our grasp, we tend to ignore or let go. Why was this sticking to her, the way those field burrs used to stick to Laura and Sherrie's clothes, after a long day of playing outdoors?

The burrs, Laura's mother had once explained, were the never-give-up kind of seed that would find a way to get where they were going, and where they were going didn't matter so much to them, as long as it meant new purple thistles come next year. Before they got the privilege of becoming purple again, they paraded in a tenacious kind of unassuming brown—hundreds of little crochet-hook type heads finding their way onto dog fur or children's socks. Thistles weren't fussy.

For as long as she could remember, Laura had always seen novels as a fussy thing. It probably came of having to read books like *Lord of the Flies* and *Moby-Dick*, that were set before students as classics to pick apart, analyze, and understand as models of great writing.

This complicated matters for someone like Laura, because it made her anxious. If she was going to write a novel, she felt defeated before she began, because someone might be coming along to pick it apart, looking for symbols like The Conch or The Whale, which seemed to have mythic proportions.

Laura had seen a poetry review not long ago, where a big literary critic had downgraded a promising new poet's collection for not being mythic enough. At one level, Laura could care less about being mythic; on another level, she wondered if this is what would set a writer apart from someone like Pynchon. All of it was confusing, in its way. Maybe the act of storytelling itself was mythic enough—part of the common heritage of humanity. But writers like Melville didn't seem to think so. They spent a lot of time and a lot of pages filled with symbols, to ultimately say "mythic."

Writers like Melville, it seemed to Laura, were on to something, but it felt too forced for her taste, like the writers were trying to make their mythic point and the reader couldn't escape thinking about it, all the while feeling themselves to be like that poor Conch or The Whale, handled or hunted.

One thing Laura loved about Geoffrey was how he really had no patience for poems that seemed to be telling you, "I am a great and respectable poem, worthy of being picked apart in English class." Not that the poems he liked weren't worthy. It was a fine line.

Angry as she felt towards Geoffrey, she could give him this: She'd always felt free to write crap for him, because he didn't see it that way. He'd appreciated the way she joined deep human emotion to the simplest things—a cup, a seashell, a few scattered tea leaves.

It was strange, really, because Geoffrey could be antagonistic in his approach in the classroom (she'd witnessed this a few times, having slipped in, at his invitation, to hear him lecture). Yet his antagonism did not manifest itself in how he read simple poems. She'd understood this almost from the start, when, after she'd sent him her sestina "The Proposal," he'd sent along a poem by Jim Harrison, called "Word Drunk." It was about a poet whose whoring was actually in his perfection and unwillingness to be prolific like Li Po and his twenty thousand poems, for fear of not winning prizes and grants.

After reading Harrison's poem, Laura understood what Geoffrey might want from her—more and more and more poems, and not so much worrying about getting things "right." It had felt freeing, and she'd taken up the invitation, somewhere deep inside, and told him as much in a poem called "Li Po."

1

Li Po knew
the fecund trees
full of blossoms,
the tea bushes
flush with leaves,
sweet scent rising
from snow-petaled earth,
spears rolled–or broken–
between fingers and thumb

2

Every morning
I am Li Po,
if only I hear
the expectant cup

3

And if the porcelain overturns,
what then?

4

the snow-petaled earth
the snow-petaled earth

Thinking of Geoffrey's generosity as a reader, Laura suddenly missed him. He'd been her porcelain cup, hadn't he? Damn him, she thought. It wasn't fair. With Megan's challenge on the table, she needed him now.

A writer is always writing for someone. Laura had seen that posted somewhere online, in big black letters on a white background, as if in its starkness it was a foregone conclusion. Maybe it was.

She'd known the power, at least, of writing for Geoffrey and had gone a long way towards Li Po's 20,000 poems, sometimes composing ten or more poems in a single day, for over two years. He had read them all. "Keep sending," he'd say, if she suddenly got shy and felt she was burdening him with her words.

Laura had friends who took months, even years, to write poems. These people were good poets, published poets. But she didn't have the patience for such an approach. To her, a poem was like dialog—something you'd speak until you needed to say something else altogether different. She'd always wished that Geoffrey would have spoken back with poems of his own, but this wasn't how it went. His silence in this way didn't seem to stop the outpouring of her words.

So it surprised Laura when her words choked after Geoffrey was gone. Like a conversation suspended in mid-air, the possibility of an answer truly eclipsed, she could not speak poems for a long time.

It was Twitter that had brought her back into poetic conversation. She couldn't remember how she'd gotten involved, but she'd discovered a group of people who held poetry parties, writing together for an hour straight, weaving and reweaving each other's words. It was fast, crazy fun—a chance to write for someone, so to speak, after which you could disappear. She always did. Until Megan.

"You and me, on a subtle base of Ceylon and China teas," Laura had tweeted one night at a party, almost a year ago now. Megan had promptly retweeted and followed her.

"We've got a Ceylon and China with tones of peach and strawberry."

"Oh?" Laura had interrupted her poem-tweeting to answer Megan.

"Yup. Even has sunflower petals. A French delight!"

Laura had clicked over to Megan's profile after the party and followed her. This took Laura to the *Tea for Two* website, where she looked up the Ceylon and China and placed an order. When the tea came in its silver striped, matte-finish packet, with a little plum seal, she knew she'd come into something lasting. Her cabinet was now filled with assorted *Tea for Two* selections, each with its own poem quote on the back. What a marvelous idea; tea and poetry together seemed apt.

Somewhere along the year of getting to know Megan in boxes of 140 characters, Laura had tweeted out a teacup poem in pieces.

"I want your cup poem for my website," Megan had DM'ed her. "Does that work for you?"

Yes, it would work for Laura. And so, after an exchange of email addresses, Laura had sent the poem along in its proper form. Megan put it on her site for a few weeks; she was always in the market for tea poems or cup poems, to promote the tea-as-poetry-and-connection idea that was the foundation for *Tea for Two*.

Laura rather liked the poem for its ambiguity-of-address. It seemed to be both a statement and a question. It might have been written to someone real or someone she only wished was real…

Dear—

1

What if

2

What if the only way
she could write again
required a white cup

3

And the cup,
would she pour herself
into it? Or, rather, bring it to her lips.

4

What if

5

What if she held the cup very close,
by its delicate white handle,
and whispered into the hollow.

6

Something like—
I was five, and he said
pick mulberries with me;
I could show you the tree
on which they weep and sway.
And her mother held her chin
and said, *tell him no...*
it would spoil your hand-sewn dress.

Thinking on the poem again, Laura realized how unusual Megan really was. It took a person of a special kind of vision to put something like that on her website. It was no Hallmark poem, for sure. Megan had run the poem next to a haunting photo by Kelly Sauer: a woman in a white dress, lying on the ground, covered with rose petals beneath a weeping tree, her feet bare and somehow sorrowful, if one's feet could be such a thing.

Next to the woman image, there was a photo of a blue roses cup filled with loose French tea. Laura had actually ordered the mulberry blend. If she ended up finding her tea basket before midnight, she might even steep it and bring it out here, to sip quietly under the rising moon.

17

"What should I write about?" Laura decided to challenge Megan; why should the challenge only go one way?

"Your father. Everybody does," Megan had tweeted without hesitation.

By now, the night dew had settled. Laura could feel it in the air, and the first soft sounds of crickets were moving over the yard. A Luna moth had joined the lesser, nameless moths still circling the porch lamp. Her mother had taught her to recognize their delicate green and to know that a fuller set of antennae indicated a male. This one was a female.

You could use a moth like that as a symbol in a novel, but it was trite, wasn't it? The old moth-to-the-flame image had been used and used again. It was the stuff of amateur poetry. And she, having so little experience crafting a story, would be the most in danger of falling into trite approaches. If she wrote a novel, it probably would be about her father. And the male Luna moth would haunt its pages. Everyone would recognize the work as that of a first novelist. "She wrote about herself through the lens of her father."

The really good novelists, Laura thought, put their fathers, and maybe their mothers too, deeper into the stories. Which, she suddenly thought, might redeem Melville just the littlest bit. Maybe the whale was his father and it was a kind of Freudian treatment, an Oedipal thing. You could pull this off better with a whale, perhaps, than by writing about a flesh-and-blood man.

On the other hand, there was Wendell Berry, putting the father front and center in *Nathan Coulter,* where he fought his son with the ferocity of Melville's whale and kept escaping, at least for a time.

Or maybe, she thought, you could take both approaches. A wolf could be someone you knew. A man who drove a woman into the mountains to conceive a daughter could also be someone you knew. Both could be your father. Or both could be someone else altogether—a client, maybe, who had taken you for a ride. It didn't matter, did it?

The problem came, Laura thought, when you worked too hard to try to make these things happen, instead of letting them unfold.

Geoffrey had asked her once, about how she wrote poetry. Where did she begin? "I start anywhere," she'd said, which was mostly true. The truer truth was that she always began with an emotion—sorrow, desire, love, anger. The emotion was like Shelley's Frankenstein, desperately wandering the frozen landscape, until it found a crack in the ice, through which it could slip down, down, to where it was dark and warm, to the place where images were sleeping and waiting to be wakened. So, yes, maybe she'd feel sadness and write to Geoffrey about seashells. But the poem was really about the sadness…

> Do the shells still hear the sea,
> though they are in pieces;
> how deep does the hearing of the sea
> enter into bone...

Poets, thought Laura, were used to this game of animating the image. Sometimes their creations were a bit Frankenstein, a malformed piecing together, but the good poet did not lose hope. There was always the possibility of being a different kind of creator, more like the one pictured in the old stories of Genesis. A being who hovered over chaos, to bring form and light. A being who could play in the dust and breathe something astonishing into body and soul.

And poets knew all the tricks of animation. They knew that your father could be a Luna moth or even the icy landscape that

Frankenstein traversed.

Laura looked around her and thought the whole porch, the drawers and cabinets inside the house, the back yard, contained enough to give her a thousand novels. She could start anywhere. The white pine, the lemon chair she'd tossed because Geoffrey said it was old and not worth keeping, the card table someone else had discarded but which she now leaned across to tweet to Megan. There were stories everywhere.

Maybe the real problem wasn't that she had nothing to write about, but that she had too much. Maybe she wasn't afraid of her finiteness after all, but rather Infinity and how it called her to begin somewhere, anywhere. To begin might be an acceptance that indeed she was some kind of creator, with tremendous powers. It might mean taking people's lives into her hands—her own life, her friends', even her father's or mother's. And maybe she was afraid they would think she had animated a wandering Frankenstein no one wanted to hold.

18

"Search inside this book."

Laura clicked through to check out Nancy Kress's *Characters, Emotion & Viewpoint*. The title itself had already made her feel daunted. Was writing a novel going to require an ability to juggle all the formulas at once? A simple title like *Character* would have settled her better.

She scanned the Table of Contents, and her heart sank a little more. *What do readers want? The Motivationally Complicated Character. Showing Change in Your Characters. Omniscient Point of View.* These breakdowns of how a novel's characters could be strengthened must have helped someone, or the book wouldn't be 13,000-in-books on the seller's website, would it? Laura clicked away to start another chat with James. It was getting late now, and the first stars had appeared over the white pine. He might have shut down for the night. She hoped not.

"Have you ever written about your father, James? I mean, in your poems? Is he hiding somewhere in the lines?"

The chat box remained empty. Oh, James, Laura thought. Where are you? Toothbrushing at a time like this?

After Laura had written "The Proposal" sestina for James, he'd sent along a digital copy of his first poetry book *The Whole Truth*. Laura had actually been shocked by the aggression and anger that shot through the poems, making sestinas into something she'd not yet experienced: a kind of punching dialog that could knock through you rather than roll along lyrically and lull you almost into denial.

She'd written a few sestinas besides the one she sent to James, and hers were all a slow drowning into emotion, caused by the rolling repetition of the end words and the overall internal sounds. When it became clear to Laura that she was really going to lose Geoffrey, for instance, she'd written "Petit à Petit L'Oiseau Fait Son Nid."

Little by little, they say,
the bird makes its nest.
I have been making mine
in silvered hemlocks, time
after time; today I used a red
thread I found near the garden.

I used to dream of living in a garden,
listening to words white orchids say
to emerald hummingbirds, red-
throated, stealing gold for nests
the size of women's thimbles, time
beating between breaths, a rhythm mine

could never find trapped, as in a mine
long hollowed, tapped black garden
that metamorphosed over time,
caught sounds of earth-on-earth say,
Come bed yourself on rock-hard nest,
turn death to sapphire, diamond, ruby red.

Rumor spreads: inside the earth is red,
molten, thrusting gold like mine
into the sun, into evening's nest
that sits above an empty garden
where orchids do not say
it is time

it is time
to ravel rays from ravished dreams, red
and unremembered; it is time to say
what is yours and what is mine

it is time to turn the garden
into earth, find fool's gold for a nest.

I have been making such a nest,
little by little, time after time,
I have been dreaming near a garden
in threads of memories, ruby red.
I have been claiming what is mine
and inviting you to say

you want the nest, the gold turning red,
the time we knew was mine,
the garden waiting, for what you have to say.

That was the thing about Laura. She walked on the border of denial even as she seemed to press forward, despite herself, through poetic words. The truth, if she kept writing poems, would always eventually surface like rubies and gold, even if the truth was that she had drowned.

Maybe James had written his truths into the angry, lascivious courtroom scenes of his sestinas. Maybe this had been his golden key to a new personality. Because, though he sometimes teased her with an edgy tone, James was a different man than he'd been. She felt this deep down, in his tender ways towards her—the mix of fatherly care and a lover's aching hope for her future.

"Yes."

The chat box jumped, with the addition of this one little word from James.

"Yes, you are brushing your teeth, while I am in writer's crisis over here?" she typed and added a winky.

"No."

"No, you aren't brushing your teeth? That's not good oral

practice, James."

"Yes, I've written about my father."

Laura sat very still, and tears began to well up.

"I know," she typed. "We have all written about our fathers, or wanted to. You are very brave."

The chat box sat empty for a long moment, and Laura looked out over the lawn, its gentle incline now silvering with the risen moon.

"I love you, Laura," the chat window slid up.

Laura stared at these three little words, so small against the whiteness of the chat box. And she knew it was true, this love. Not that it mattered. Their difference in age, their separate geographies.

"ILY2," she typed.

"What's that? Speaking in code? Have you turned into a secret agent on me?" James could never be serious for long.

"I have," she returned. "Love is the greatest secret."

19

Laura closed the laptop and let her mind drift. Maybe she could fool Megan with pieces of a story. Others had done it. That Barkat woman, one reviewer said, had added a lot of blank pages to her book, to make it look bigger, to fool her readers into thinking they'd gotten the whole story.

At least one astute person had seen through the trick, while another had praised Barkat for the blanks, saying they were a clever addition as journal pages for readers to bring their own stories to the book—so apt for a very personal work on writing. Laura had read Barkat's amused response in an interview, when Barkat had been presented with these conflicting opinions. "Oh? The blanks were just my publisher's design decision. To visually separate chapters." She'd gone on, and Laura found this intriguing, "Funny how our pre-cognitive commitments about an author will color our interpretation of what she does next."

Did Megan have pre-cognitive commitments about Laura? If so, how deep did they go? Would Laura be able to find a story that would not trespass those ideas too deeply? And what if she could not? Writing for someone seemed to be such a dangerous gamble.

She got up from the table now and stepped over to the little herb garden. The spiny rosemary, flowy and reaching like some kind of seaweed, had survived the winter, since Laura had let maple leaves gather around its base in a protective circle. The chives nearby were long and slender, just coming into lavender flower. You could eat those blooms, and sometimes she plucked them whole, then broke them between finger and thumb over her salad, releasing their onion sweetness.

The edge of the garden was lined with small conch shells— none of them whole. She squatted down to run her fingers over their backs. Ridged, they were, and layered with dirt. She picked one up and traced the sharp lines of its brokenness. The little point at the tip looked like a fine nipple. Geez, Pynchon was even in her garden.

Turning the shell, she raised it to her cheek and felt the coolness against her skin. The sea. It was there, wasn't it? Somewhere in the remnant. She tipped the shell to her ear, but it had been broken open so far that all she could hear was the sound of crickets rising everywhere around her.

A memory began to form, or re-form, of that day she'd gone sailing with her father and stepmother. They'd gotten up very early and sailed all day, going far, far from shore and finding a little island to explore. Her stepmother had packed a lot of liverwurst sandwiches, and Laura had eaten one that had mustard. Later that night, her stepmother probably tired from the day, the balance of the sandwiches was put on the table for dinner. But these liverwursts had mayonnaise.

"My mom says it's bad to eat mayonnaise if it's sat in the sun," Laura had announced.

"That's your dinner."

"But my mom said—"

"Eat it or go hungry."

Laura had gone hungry. It was a double risk (she knew from her mother) to eat a lunchmeat with mayonnaise that had sat all day in the heat. You could get really sick. People had died from such things.

A few lines from Adrienne Rich now rose in Laura's consciousness. Geoffrey had given her Rich's book *The Dream of a Common Language,* and this set of lines from the Twenty-One Love Poems section had pressed itself into her...

I touch you knowing we weren't born tomorrow,

and somehow, each of us will help the other live,
and somewhere, each of us must help the other die.

Laura had refused to die that day, after sailing. Instead, she went to bed hungry. She refused to die the next day at breakfast, when the sandwiches returned, their inner sickness now having seeped into the soggy white bread. She refused to die again at lunchtime. And finally her stepmother, perhaps fearing that Laura actually would make herself sick from not eating, relented and threw the sandwiches away.

Laura held the seashell against her chest now, as if it was a thing being born. When had she lost the ability to defend herself? When had she unlearned how to stand up (or sit down) for herself?

It was true, what Adrienne Rich said. *We weren't born tomorrow.* Time was short, in its way. The only time to be born, on any given day, was today. She fingered the shell and moved it closer to her heart.

Each of us will help the other live. That came before the final line. It must come, mustn't it? Laura-the-child had known this. Known she wasn't ready for the end of the poem. Known who to turn to, even if that person wasn't in her presence, to find the help to live.

Laura raised the broken shell to her lips and faced into the deepening night. "Thank you, James," she whispered. And the crickets kept on with their songs.

20

"How's my novel coming?" Megan tweeted to Laura. Was she going to keep this up in front of the crowd of 100,000? Of course she was, Laura thought. *That's Megan. Happily perseverant.*

Laura ignored the tweet and typed **wordcandy.me** into her internet address bar. The WordCandy web app was a cool place to find quotes. You could use it say things to people. Anything from love-sentiments to encouragements. Laura thought maybe she could use it now, to have this conversation with Megan through "candy" instead of a straight tweet. There was a category, she seemed to remember, called *Write It, Sugar,* and this might have what she needed.

The WordCandy page loaded and three category buttons popped up: *Red Hot Licorice, Lemon Primrose Love,* and *Kisses, Oh Kisses.* Not exactly the right candy for the occasion. She refreshed the screen a few times, each time trying to wish the random app onto her side. *Come on, I need a way to answer Megan.* Finally, the buttons appeared in a surprising trinity of what she needed—*Courage Candy, Hope Confections,* and *Write It, Sugar.*

She clicked on *Write It, Sugar* and a quote popped up: *We contain fields upon fields of stories.* Hmmm. Megan would jump on that one. No, she needed something different. Laura clicked *Re-Candy Me!* and went through quote after quote from Stephen King, Tim O'Brien, Mark Twain, until she found the perfect line: *Writing takes time.* A little link under the quote noted it was from *Rumors of Water.* She should probably read the book, had heard it was pretty good. But at the moment, Barkat's book was giving her everything she needed—a simple talkback to Megan.

Laura clicked through the rest of the candy process, "wrapping" the quote on a gorgeous photo that looked to be a Claire Burge. Claire was a WordCandy photographer and entrepreneur who Laura also followed on Twitter. Full of energy and dreams, she seemed like a person who could make anything happen, or make you believe that *you* could make anything happen. She exuded the kind of strength Laura needed to answer Megan.

Laura pressed the thumbnail of *Writing takes time,* now set against the purple-blue photograph of a road at eye level, and the app took her to another page where she tweeted the beautiful quote to *@meganwillow.*

When Laura had come back to the porch, she'd brought the conch shell and placed it on the table next to her laptop. She traced its silhouette now and thought about Megan's last name. *Willow.*

After Laura's father had left, Cora remarried to a man who was difficult in so many ways. It was in this man's household that Laura's new stepbrother had abused her briefly, until she'd asked her mom if it was okay for a boy to do certain things with his fingers, and Cora had told her these were dirty ways of touching and she would get an infection. Laura had announced to the son, then, that she preferred not to play "the game" anymore, and he had stopped—but not before Laura had learned a strange mix of excitement, fear, and shame about sex, that seemed to have carried right through to adulthood. And maybe, she thought now, it had carried through not just about physical intimacy but about anything that promised to open her.

Her stepbrother was definitely the offspring of his father, who had pushed the boundaries of Laura's vulnerabilities. When, in middle school, she had begun developing young-girl breasts that first appeared as little *v*'s, her stepfather had taken every opportunity to talk about *tits* and how someday Laura would be showing them to everybody, maybe even like the strippers he went to watch on Friday nights, or maybe just to all the boys in backseats and haylofts. And, he'd always added, she'd be "knocked up" by the age of sixteen and never amount to anything. These predictions had bred in her a careful determination to never get pregnant, and to this day she never had.

Inexplicably, it was her stepfather who had planted her favorite tree as an anniversary present for Laura's mom. It stood by the pond where Laura and Sherrie spent many a summer day squishing into the mud, their toes nibbled by catfish. The tree was a willow that, over the years, grew tall and graceful, its long tendrils weeping over Laura, into the water. When she'd finally moved on from that place and, against all odds, gone to college, she had wished she could take the willow with her.

Well, she had the pine now, which was something. And, she smiled to herself, she had this crazy friend Megan Willow, who seemed not so much to be weeping over Laura as to be laughing and carrying on.

"Writing takes time. That's not what Barkat meant," Megan had now tweeted. "I've read the book."

Damn that Megan. Had she read every book? Did she know everything? Could Laura do nothing to get around her?

"I think she meant no novel by September."

"Nope," tweeted Megan.

"Okay, dear Empress. Do explicate Barkat."

"She meant you have to live a story for a time."

"And?"

"And then you can write it, in time. What have you lived?"

"Kind of a personal question for Twitterland."

"Kind of the perfect question to answer in fiction."

This seemed plausible. Tim O'Brien had played with the concept, writing a novel about the war, after being in the war. He even wrote it in first person, as if he was the fictional character. Then he played with the idea of story all the way through, teasing the reader to wonder what he had lived and what was total bullshit.

Laura had raised the issue once with James, about how fiction skated the line between truth and lies. But James had told her it was all the same thing; even if a story was a flat-out lie, it was true "by my lights." He had said that—*by my lights*—and this had made Laura smile, because she didn't know anyone who used that expression and for some reason it reminded her of the Northern Lights and the stars.

She looked out over the yard now, wishing the urban glare of her small city didn't obscure the night sky so much. If only she could see the Big Dipper pouring, she might feel like James was somehow up there, shining down wisdom, encouraging her to lie her way to the truth, in time.

21

It was a short book. Laura knew that from the reviews. If she downloaded it right now, she could probably finish it before midnight and still have time for tea. Mondays were a rush at the agency where she worked, but one Monday seen through sleepy eyes wasn't going to kill her. She could stay up and hopefully find some much-needed writing advice to meet Megan's challenge.

Laura clicked over to the bookseller and searched for *Rumors of Water*. A few selections popped up, all books of Barkat's. There it was. The one with the empty teacup on the cover. She bought it, and this time she ignored the offer to tweet her purchase to the world. It wouldn't do to have Megan see this.

"I don't feel like I've finished living that enough," Barkat was explaining to her friend Anne, making excuses about why she couldn't write about life with her daughters.

Yup, Laura mentally agreed.

"...this is both true and not true at all," Barkat continued.

Shit, thought Laura. Maybe this was not going to be the help she needed after all. She should go in the house and make a better effort to find the tea basket.

If I was a tea basket, where would I hide? Laura amused herself with such imaginations, when looking for lost things. Sometimes it worked. She'd found the Adrienne Rich volume from Geoffrey this way. After he'd been gone for a while and she was searching for a poem quote...

> *I dreamed you were a poem,*
> I say, *a poem I wanted to show someone*

There had been a time when she wanted to show Geoffrey to everyone. He was charming and very smart, confident in ways

Laura only wished she could be. But when she'd "shown" Geoffrey to her mother, it hadn't gone particularly well on either side. Laura could tell through her mother's body language, by the end of the visit, that somehow Geoffrey had closed something between him and her or even between Laura and her mother.

And then, of course, there'd been Geoffrey's comment on the way home, insulting Cora, though Laura herself hadn't seen it like that at the time. In fact, she realized now, she'd even laughed along, which made her wonder who had actually done the closing between her and her mother—Geoffrey or Laura.

There'd been a time, too, when Geoffrey had wanted to show Laura to everyone. He thought she was as sexy as her poems, at least at first. But over time, the simplicity of her sensuality had no longer seemed to shine through to him. He'd taken to buying her "better clothes" and recommended that maybe she consult with his graduate assistant, Alicia, who had excellent taste in fashion and could surely advise Laura on how to put herself together for a stronger overall effect.

Perhaps this was why Laura had lost the Adrienne Rich volume, because she had not seemed to be a poem to Geoffrey anymore, and she didn't need to be reading words that reminded her of this reality. At least, it occurred to Laura now, this was a possible reason for Adrienne going missing. Maybe people lost things because the things themselves were signs of what was being avoided or what was no longer needed or any combination of realities that buried themselves in the disappearance or appearance of actual items in a person's environment.

Geoffrey, for instance, had lost the strip of plum silk she'd trimmed from her cami and sent to him, pressed between ivory sheets of a poem called "Estrella"...

Sometimes when the night comes on

and Venus rises bright over the river,

I think I can see a boat floating white
in the mist, and my heart opens

with a fainting motion, laying back
on its bed of flesh.

Oh, to see the boat, going its way
towards the great, unfathomable sea.

He'd kept the silken plum strip in his wallet, where he said it would
peek out at him like an unjaded treasure amidst the symbols of
commerce and worldliness—dollars, credit cards, his Yale ID.

Then one day the plum was gone. He'd mentioned that over
a Bagatelle tea. And Laura knew now that she should have understood it as the portent it was, and that the poem she had pressed
it into would take on another meaning, too. The little boat would
not be coming to her as Venus rose over the river, but would,
in fact, make its way to the great unfathomable sea, while she
remained adrift in the white sheets of her own empty bed.

22

If the tea basket was not going to reveal its whereabouts, not even in Laura's imagination, she might as well move along and pull out the kettle. Sometimes you had to push through, didn't you? Even if you didn't have the tools to accompany you on your way? Something would appear. An idea, a different tool, a woodsman bearing rescue tea equipment. She laughed to herself, to think of Red Riding Hood's face-the-wolf dilemma being solvable by tea and biscuits.

Laura's mother could probably quell a wolf with tea and a diversionary pastry. As Laura recalled, Cora had solved so many problems over the years, through unexpected means, perhaps drawing on the creative mischief she'd developed as a child during her own mother's absences.

Cora-the-child's cooking skills, for instance, had involved the milkman. Every day, he'd leave fresh bottles of milk in a little wooden box on their doorstep, and sometimes Cora would sneak some for her mud pies.

"Oh, the mud pies were delicious and nutritious, at least for the robins!" Laura's mother would retell the stories of stealing her mother's pie pans and filling them with dirt, illicit milk, blackberries, and eggs she'd snatch from the chickens' hideaways. The recipe changed by season and available ingredients. Now milkweed seeds, now thistles. Wild blueberries or apples from the orchard—the one that was eventually lost to a tornado. Laura's mother had hidden in the root cellar when she saw the tornado coming on grey and terrifying, funneling its way through generations of plantings that, when she emerged from underground, were all uprooted and tipped to the sky.

It was stories like these that Cora would tell on days they'd sneak time together cooking—Cora and Laura and Sherrie, in the kitchen of her stepfather, where the girls were not welcome because, he said, they were filthy pigs not fit to touch his dishes (or the pie pans, or the muffin pans, for that matter).

Cora would wait until Laura's stepfather left the house for his hunting. Then she'd pull out the eggs and milk, the flour and oil, sugar and a few overripe bananas, and they'd begin. Mashing, sifting, mixing. All the while, Cora telling stories.

"We did! Took the screen door right off its hinges. Strained vegetable soup into a pot on the living room floor. We didn't like the vegetables."

Laura and Sherrie's eyes would grow wide at the audacity of the thing. Could it be true that this tiny woman, flour on her purple t-shirt and streaks of new-grey in her hair, had helped de-hinge a screen door because she and her sister couldn't find their mother's strainer?

"That's nothing," Cora would say. "We washed it up and put the screen door back when we were through. But when we cut the fringes off the bottom of the couch, we got a whipping. Well, because there was no way to hide the evidence of that."

Then Cora would laugh, and Laura and Sherrie would laugh, and nothing would matter in that moment. Just the stories and their mother shining.

There must be more stories like these, Laura thought now. It wasn't possible that Cora's mischief had been confined to mud pies and a screen door, a single de-fringed couch. Why had Laura never taken the time to delve deeper into the life of her mother? Chickens. An orchard. These spoke of the possibility of a farm. But Laura's memories of her mother's childhood were skewed in one direction: her own memories of her grandmother's house near a highway, with a nothing-of-a-driveway and a dark kitchen with white Formica countertops. This could not be the house of Cora's childhood, but Laura had never pushed beyond it.

Geoffrey had called Laura his Murasaki, that first night together, but she knew now that this naming was beyond generous. A vision, perhaps in spite of himself, of a Laura that had not yet existed.

Murasaki had written into her own tales the failure of imagination Laura had demonstrated. In a delightful exchange Murasaki could pull off because it was in story form, the Japanese tale-weaver had arranged a naughty retort from a young girl to an important male character, Genji.

Genji had found this girl, Tamakazura, copying out yet another tale, hoping to find among its extraordinary fates, one like her own. He'd exclaimed to the girl, "Oh, no, this will never do! Women are obviously born to be fooled without a murmur of protest. There is hardly a word of truth in all of this, as you know perfectly well." He had laughed at her then and gone on about the idle persuasiveness of the "glib imagination."

Tamakazura had replied simply, "Yes, of course, for various reasons someone accustomed to telling lies will no doubt take tales that way," and she asserted that she herself couldn't see them as anything but true.

When confronted with his failure of imagination, Genji had backed off and changed his argument, saying that the *Chronicles of Japan,* the official history, really only gave part of the truth. It had tickled Laura when Murasaki's narrator concluded that Genji "mounted a very fine defense of tales."

Standing here now, filling the kettle, Laura realized she was no Murasaki, no Tamakazura. She had failed to seek her mother's tales and copy them out with expectation and hope. Yes, Geoffrey had been generous to call her Murasaki, whether or not he understood that.

Laura's eyes filled with tears, and she set the kettle on the stove.

23

Electric oven, gas range. Laura's stove was a combination deal. She loved the little snapping sound of the starters that would ignite the flames, but now she paused before turning the front-burner knob. She should pick a tea, figure a method for steeping, dry her tears.

Tea was more than boiling water. There were decisions to be made and a frame of mind to develop, no matter how imperceptible. It was like Megan had emphasized to Sophia when they were first brainstorming about *Tea for Two*.

Sophia had what Megan called "tea mind," a strong belief in the power of tea to transport a person outside herself, to allow her to encounter the inner truth of things, no matter how imperfect they might seem at first. Sophia was all about bringing this experience to customers, on a philosophical level. Megan was about making it happen through strategy and hard work. "In my opinion, all things are born to thrive," she'd written to Sophia. "You cannot go wrong when you create something, be it a life or a business, if you take responsibility to see that it thrives."

To Laura, this seemed sensible enough, and true, but maybe a little trickier than Megan had made it seem. Making something thrive might require things of you that caused other things not to thrive. There could be a conflict, as it were, of born-things surviving.

She thought back now to the hanging tree—an old maple, long dead, that had stood beside their long, dirt driveway when she was a child. Money had been scarce, the alimony from her father often not arriving for months, and her stepfather's means of making a living (siding and roofing) being dependent on the weather.

So her stepfather had provided for them by hunting more than his share. He'd bring home deer in the back of the blue pickup, then hang them from the maple to drain their lifeblood before beginning the butchering process. Laura's own mother had helped out on the back porch, skinning the gentle tawny creatures, quartering and chopping and wrapping the meat into thick white paper, then tying it with a heavy string.

Sometimes when Laura's stepfather had overstepped his hunting quota, and he needed to hide the evidence from the local authorities, he and his sons would hang the extra deer in the old cellar under her mother's garden. If you walked around and down the hill, you could gain access to this dark place through a door with a rusty handle.

Times when there were no deer hanging from the big iron ceiling hooks, Laura and Sherrie were made to each take a broom and sweep up the dried blood and mud the men's boots had left on the broken concrete. Once, while sweeping, she and Sherrie found an old hand drill shaped like a T, with an enormous spiral head that came to a sharp point. Laura, the eldest, had claimed first dibs on trying to screw the drill into a crack. They would dig all the way to China, they'd agreed, starting with this unassuming opening.

When Laura seemed ineffective and perhaps had taken more than her share of time, Sherrie had grabbed the drill and jabbed it to Laura's chest. "I'll kill you!" she'd screamed, and somehow Laura had thought she really might. She'd run out of the cellar, shouting for her mother to save her. As it turned out, her mother must have done so, though Laura could no longer remember the details of what followed. At the very least, she figured Sherrie must have secured a few moments to herself, in which she could take the pleasure of finding a crack and, through the force of her own weight and turning, make an entry to the earth.

Now, Laura pulled a tissue from the box at the back of the counter and wiped her tears. Sherrie had really been something, hadn't she. And it was Sherrie whose small braveries seemed to extend right out to her imagination and the will to set it down. Laura could remember how Sherrie would sit for hours, pencil to notebook, making story after story, filling page after page. Then Sherrie would call her into their room and they'd pull the bed sheets over them, to make a shadowy cave, and Sherrie would read her tales about all the usual things—princesses and Indians, wild horses and talking mice.

Laura herself had been afraid to imagine, always getting stuck on beginnings and trying to perfect them. Like Megan's partner Sophia, who'd been filled with the magical lure of tea-mind, Laura had overflowed with the deep enchantment of story-mind. She knew what she hoped to bring a reader—yes, the transport outside oneself, the encounter with the inner truth of things. Not that she'd conceived of it quite that way as a child, but she'd understood the power of what Sherrie so bravely took into her hands, so she could find the crevices that led to a listener's heart.

Opening the cabinet under the sink, Laura leaned down to toss away her tear-stained tissue. What had it taken for Sherrie to make a story thrive, she wondered. What secret might it require Laura to pierce, standing here now.

24

There comes a time when you should walk away. Laura knew that, but she'd never been particularly good at it. With her and Geoffrey, that time had probably been the night of the frog cup.

The cup was such a stupid thing, really. A leftover from childhood. Laura and Sherrie used to fight over the cup. Plain ivory, with a ceramic frog stuck to its inside bottom. Laura's mom had always tried to monitor whose turn it was to use it, but this never stopped a tiff from arising, over who would get the pure delight of surprise after Cora had steeped Lipton tea in the cup and added a pour of milk. Laura herself had always tried to prolong the experience, sipping as slowly as possible, before she'd be met with the big circles of white and black frogeyes and the green tip of a nose.

She and Geoffrey had been making *matcha,* a powdered Japanese tea, and Laura had perhaps unwisely chosen the frog cup from her cabinet. Geoffrey preferred the Princeton she'd bought in a small set at the outlet store. It was fine white china with a navy and gold rim. She wasn't sure if his enduring affection for the cup had more to do with its fine lines or the poem she'd sent him after he used it the first time...

> This morning, in the sunset yellow dining room,
> I held the Princeton to my lips, its handle soft
> between my thumb and tiny index finger,
> its gold rim imperceptible to taste, but circling
> nonetheless.
>
> Lazy, perhaps, or careless, I had seated the Princeton
> in the Profile saucer (also white, also fine bone). Still.
> When I held it close, and towards the light, my left hand
> joining the embrace, I thought to ask you this:

Did you know, if you tilt the bone just right,
you can see the fingers silhouetted, on the other side.

The poem had earned her a date at The Inn at 56 Irving, a bed and
breakfast establishment in New York City. The Inn was filled with
antiques, dark wood trim, and marble fireplaces. A paper mâché
chess set was displayed in the small living room where guests could
play, should they wish to, before slinking away to their downy
duvets and a complimentary glass of champagne.

Geoffrey had challenged her to a game of chess that night,
and he'd beaten her soundly. She'd never been good at chess anyway and the distraction of the plum and gold hand-painted board
and the intricate lacquered pieces had only assured she would play
worse than ever.

He had found it amusing that she didn't have a head for chess.
Later, when they'd stripped down to their naked selves, and she
was in his arms, he teased her for her loss. "Making up stories
while you played, I bet," he said. "Just like your sweet little mother.
You can't win a game like that, Laura. It makes you vulnerable to
the thinking man."

She'd kissed his mouth to stop the words, but the words had
obviously stayed with her. Just as the night of the frog cup had
stayed with her, for what seemed like far too long.

Laura opened her cabinet now and ran her finger along the
ivory wooden shelf. This was where she'd kept the cup, having
packed it and moved it from dorm room to apartment to apartment and finally to this house, carrying it forward since childhood.
How she'd managed to secure the cup for her own was a bit of a
mystery now, but she'd done it. Then came the night of the *matcha*.

She'd planned to lightly stir the powder around the frog, with
the use of a wooden chopstick. It would be like the frog had his
own little green pond, and she'd be a girl simply dipping in her

toes. But Geoffrey had stepped between her and the cup, sporting a silver spoon he'd found in her special utensils drawer. The spoon was too large, or the force of his hand too great, and within moments he had accidentally beheaded the frog with a loud "clink."

"Damn it," he'd said, and tipped the *matcha* out to see the evidence of his breaking. "Probably time for this creature to return to mud anyway," Geoffrey had joked, and opened the cabinet door under the sink, tossing the cup into the trash with a single flourish.

She had stood there, as if struck dumb and motionless by some kind of Medusa, but a flood of thought and emotion surged inside her body. It was just a cup, and a ridiculous cup at that, yet she felt as if it held something larger than words could explain. Maybe it contained the moments after Cora had pulled warm banana bread from the oven—bread they'd secretly made together when her stepfather was out for the day. Cora would cut the bread with a dull knife and they'd wish for butter, but the delight of tea in the frog cup would more than make up for the lack. That seemed like a bare explanation, not nearly strong enough to justify the overwhelming sense of loss she'd felt as Geoffrey's hand discarded the simple juvenile cup. Some things could not, perhaps, be truly understood.

In that moment she'd thought to leave Geoffrey, had known somewhere deep inside that it was the right thing to do, maybe for her very life. But then he was smiling and pulling a matching Princeton from the corner cabinet. She watched his hand reach through the glass-paned door, and she could not wrest herself from the promise of the evening. *Matcha,* whisked into fresh steaming water. Poetry spoken across the dining room table.

In the morning, she had taken out the trash. And she had not bothered to retrieve the cup.

25

After Laura's father had left Cora for another woman—a nurse, the fact of which taunted Cora deeply, considering how she herself had given up her own semblance of being a nurse, to marry Laura's father—after he left, the love had drained from Cora's eyes.

Not only had the love seemed to disappear, but a hardness had set in and revealed itself in the shape of her mother's lips—a straight line that would only get straighter when the smallest things seemed to go wrong. A few incidents stood out especially, at which times the hard line of her mother's mouth had translated itself, almost like a welt, onto Laura's own being.

There'd been the time when Laura left her new birthday crayons on the old wood floor of the living room, and Cora had marched her to the burning barrel, where ordinarily they simply burned trash and broken things. Cora had gone on about Laura's misdeed, all the while dropping the waxy rainbows of possibility into the flames, one by one, and slowly, to prolong the punishment. Laura had watched in a kind of terror that seemed disproportionate to the discarding of colored wax, but there you had it: Cora seemed to be melting Laura's very soul.

Then there'd been the mud pie event, fueled by Cora's own stories of magical mud-pie making. Laura had gathered clay from one of the driveway mud puddles, thickened it with threads of grass and billows of dandelion seeds, and fed the whole concoction to Sherrie who, at age three, seemed willing to forego good taste for the chance at imagination with her big sister. Sherrie's mouth was dripping with telltale signs of mud-eating, when Cora had come out of the old white house and screamed and screamed—a series of shrieks that still echoed in Laura's consciousness, accompanied by visions of Cora's reddened face and furious eyes.

These memories were made complete by the red dress and green tights incident, when Laura had come proudly out from her room to eat her morning oatmeal before getting on the school bus. And Cora's lips had gone thin and straight. In a flat voice she'd said, "You look like a slut. Go change your clothes." Then Laura had retreated to the walk-in closet near the foot of her bed and stripped off what had seemed to her like Christmas. She put on, instead, a pair of Sears Toughskins jeans and a plain white t-shirt. You couldn't go wrong with something safe like that, she'd reasoned.

So when Laura's stepfather-to-be made Cora smile, this seemed like the stuff of happily-ever-after to Laura. She did not even remember any prolonged period of dating between the two adults. It had seemed to Laura like one day there was no man in the house and the next day she was perched on a strong knee, being asked in a deep, soothing voice, "Do you want a new daddy?"

Something inside Laura had wanted to say *no. No*, she didn't need or want a new daddy. She had a father of her own, who she expected would come back any day from wherever he had gone. But then she felt the big hands firm on her waist, and she looked up to her mother, whose eyes seemed alive and whose lips were like in the songs—red like cherries, and full. Laura had rushed through the pause of doubt, had ignored the way her body was pulling from this man, even as it was sinking into him. And that was it. "Yes," she'd said. Then Cora's smile widened, if that was possible, and their fate was sealed.

Cora had married soon after, or so it seemed in Laura's memory—as if the night of Laura's *yes* on a charming man's knee had propelled them straight into the endless drunken stupors of her stepfather, of her mother's mother's china flung across a smoke-filled kitchen, of the night her stepfather choked Sherrie almost to death. Laura's *yes*, she had learned early, was a terrible, powerful thing.

26

Murasaki had taught the Empress Chinese. Laura remembered this bit of information from the night of Geoffrey's New York lecture—the night that had ushered the two of them into months of Laura trying to write herself indelibly onto Geoffrey's heart, one isolated hotel room after another. Often, Laura would memorialize their encounter with a poem, as if the poem could make real what only lasted a night, then slipped away. She'd crafted poems about everything from the Crosby (a real splurge on Geoffrey's part) to the Seacrest that overlooked the ocean out on Long Island.

It was not proper for a Japanese woman to learn Chinese, Geoffrey had noted, much less a woman as genteel and exemplary as the Empress. But the Empress must have wanted this from Murasaki, and Murasaki had somehow obtained the knowledge for herself and she had, apparently, agreed to teach the language in secret. Laura had to smile, to think that the secret had not turned out to be so secret after all. Maybe there were letters or poems the Empress had penned in Chinese; something had revealed their bare rebellion, and Laura felt glad for it tonight. She needed, she suddenly thought, to hold on to a woman who'd said *yes* in a world of *no*'s, if she was ever going to begin her novel for Megan.

The thought of writing anything at all made her palms begin to sweat, as she stood before the open cabinet, trying to decide on a tea that would properly motivate her to begin some kind of story.

Had Mary Shelley fretted so? Maybe yes, maybe no. She'd begun her classic work on a dare. Had culled a dream to bring it into being. But it was not lost on Laura that the story might be a prolonged exercise in Shelley's personal terrors. The subtitle of the work was *Prometheus Unbound*, and Laura wondered if Shelley herself was not Prometheus in the form of the wandering monster, who desperately sought love and acceptance but was ultimately driven to face an icy landscape that seemed almost fantastical—the way our own subconscious could be, white and frozen-slippery.

The myth of Prometheus held its own fascinations. Prometheus was a tragic figure, endlessly punished for what he'd bravely done—dare to take fire into his own hands, to reveal its secrets to what he'd formed from clay: humankind, in all its neediness for something warm to console and advance it.

This is what Laura loved about literature. You could see things in it that perhaps weren't there, but might be. And even that didn't matter if, in the end, readers needed something to be there. They could bring their somethings to a text, as co-creators, embedding a needed reality in the story which, if it was flexible enough, would allow new threads to take their place beside the author's.

Thinking on Mary Shelley now, Laura could see the possibilities. Hadn't Mary's own birth been the death of her mother? How did a person live with something like that? Her mother had said *yes* to birthing and had paid with her life. Mary's existence must have been haunted by the loss and the terrible lesson. So that, perhaps her own desires to birth became all tangled and pieced, until she herself felt like the monster trying to clasp at a borrowed—no, stolen—life.

Yet Mary, in a kind of Promethean act, had bravely taken her fears and losses and woven them, thread by thread, into a story that looked nothing like her own life and beautiful figure.

Had Percy guessed he was marrying Frankenstein? Laura suspected not. Had Mary herself even known? Or was the secret kept safe from their joint consciousness, except in the writing Mary had left for the world, and which Laura now turned to with some kind of hope.

Maybe you didn't need to know anything special to write a work of fiction. Maybe you didn't need to delve into some kind of life question you knew you'd lived. Perhaps your subconscious would do the job for you, if only you dared to dream.

27

As the years had stretched on, in the house of Laura's stepfather, Cora had found ways to make things livable, if only in fleeting moments.

Laura remembered the night, for instance, of the Northern Lights—those magical flashes of rainbow that undulated from earth to heaven, in a kind of inverted funnel shape that made you feel you could travel right up its ribboned edges and find a land of dreams.

She and Sherrie had been sound asleep, when Cora had wakened them with a gentle touch and whisper, "Girls, come. I have a special secret that sometimes comes only once in a lifetime." Laura and Sherrie had believed her and roused themselves. Bare-footed, they had crept down the hall together—careful not to wake their stepfather—and had made their way onto the butchering porch.

It was just as Cora said. This was a secret worth waking for. Laura had shivered uncontrollably in the freezing December air, but the vision had sustained her. It was like nothing she'd ever seen before, nor since. Cora was right. The experience had, so far, been once in a lifetime.

In warmer seasons, Cora had taken them on long, winding walks, up the hill of the old dirt road. At the pinnacle, near the house where they'd once lived with their father, before everything had fallen apart and life had altered completely, was a tiny cottage that seemed like something from a fairy tale.

An old woman named Sarah Kipper lived in the cottage. She was wrinkled and tanned from having spent years tending her roses, which now tangled around the cottage in an unkempt patch of fragrant color. The one-room house held a bed with a peace quilt, bottles of cobalt blue and brilliant purple lined up in rows on tiny window sills, and more doilies than seemed necessary for one person to own.

Laura supposed that Sarah simply kept crocheting the doilies, in hopes she'd perhaps have someone with whom to share them—the way she also kept a rosebud plate on the table, empty and bordered by a silver fork and knife. Who were the doilies really for, Laura had always wondered as a child, and who had never come to dinner, though Sarah seemed to wait forever for his or her arrival?

The presence of Sarah's bed and its lace-edged pillows, in the same room with the table and its empty china, near an old iron sink that hung from the wall, embarrassed Laura. It was as if Sarah's secrets were too exposed, the way the woman herself exuded an obvious scent of startling, undeniable age.

There had come a day when Sarah died. Laura did not know when it had happened. She only knew that it had suddenly seemed like a long time since Cora had walked her and Sherrie up to the woman's door.

Maybe it was then that Cora had begun to find their situation no longer livable. Laura couldn't be sure. It seemed strange to think that the loss of an old woman, surrounded by doilies and roses, could spur Cora to what she finally did.

Like a character living out James Scott Bell's story-in-three-acts, Cora had turned from suicidal plans, as if walking through Door Number Two and into her own knockout ending, where she faced her greatest challenge: leaving a man who threatened to kill her if she went, but who would go on daily taking her life if she stayed.

Laura learned this only years later—how her mother had stood on the bridge behind their house and wondered if the fall would be far and powerful enough to end her life and the misery she'd married into.

But then Sarah had died, or this is how Laura suspected it went, and something about all those doilies and the still-empty plate and the roses with no one to keep them, had wakened Cora to what seemed best expressed in a line from Adrienne Rich:

> But there comes a time—perhaps this is one of them—
> when we have to take ourselves more seriously or die.

Cora had done this. Despite her often-seeming weakness, she had chosen not to jump off the bridge. Instead, she had taken the hands of her daughters. And walked over it.

28

"Canceling Marriott, NYC."

The subject line of Geoffrey's email had sat in its boldness for a whole day. Laura had not had the heart to open it, understanding somehow that this was the end she'd feared from the start.

By evening, sitting alone on her couch after the sweaty commute home, Laura had finally opened the email. It pierced her with its revelation.

As it turned out, Geoffrey's leaving had nothing to do with Russian or French, or even a woman, though his frequent flirtations with women he deemed more refined than Laura could easily have made it so.

The email said simply, "Something's come up." In an exchange that took hours to play itself out over invisible wires, Laura had learned that the something was Oxford. As in England. As in, she was not invited to go along.

Geoffrey had been courted and had accepted an offer to develop an Asian Literature program, which he felt was an intriguing direction after spending what had already seemed like too many years at Yale.

"Probably best to find some closure now, Laura," he'd written. "Not like we were going to end up in a perpetual hotel room. I thought you understood that."

"Understood that?" she'd answered.

"Understood that life moves on, Laura. In a grownup's world, this seems clearly comprehended. Opportunities come. We take them. Everybody wins if they know how to play the game. Keeps life from devolving into the tedium of your despised Pynchon."

Laura stopped searching for just the right tea now and reached for the Adrienne Rich volume Geoffrey had given her. It was sitting near the toaster, and she brushed a few crumbs off the cover before she opened it to where her bookmark had somehow come to settle itself: "Origins and History of Consciousness."

The bookmark itself was a piece of fine white paper on which Laura had scrawled her first poetic protest over Geoffrey's leaving...

Aubade

I still want you,

though it hasn't rained in forever,
and we have lost our sun umbrella.

The road is closed, the one
that leads to the sea,

where no one cares about the rain,
nor the lost umbrella,
nor these words that whisper,

wanting.

The poem to Geoffrey seemed to stand in stark contrast to the words of Adrienne that Laura now traced with her index finger...

No one lives in this room
without confronting the whiteness of the wall
behind the poems...
...

...I have dreamed of going to bed
as walking into clear water ringed by a snowy wood
white as cold sheets, thinking, *I'll freeze in there.*

My bare feet are numbed already by the snow
but the water is mild…

…

this water washes off the scent—
You are clear now
of the hunter, the trapper
the wardens of the mind—

For months after Geoffrey left, Laura had continued to send poems that somehow begged for his return. The poems, in their way, became their own walls to keep her bounded and guard her from "the whiteness of the wall behind the poems."

Occasionally, Geoffrey would send her a picture of Oxford, as if to say, "Come visit," but the images never carried any messages with them, nor any possible dates or details or the warmth of invitation.

If Geoffrey's communications had been a landscape, they would essentially have been classified as tundra—geography that only pretended at life, the way Geoffrey had perhaps pretended all along. Why he had done so, Laura wasn't sure. Maybe, like her own grandmother, he'd stayed in a relationship for the sex. And since Laura was so easy to come to and leave again, this had worked. Until he'd found a better offer.

It was James who had provided warmth through this painful period in Laura's life. After many discussions back and forth, in which Laura lamented she'd never find love again (if you could call it that), James had written to her, "I hold great hope for your future." If only she could live into that hope.

"What should I drink tonight, James?" Laura now spoke to the empty air.

She imagined the soft, sweet voice of James, giving her an

answer that was no answer at all: "I think you know what you should choose, Laura. Only one option, by my lights."

29

Wedding Imperial Tea.

Laura reached into the cabinet and pulled out the rounded black tin that held a favorite she'd received from Geoffrey. She moved to the stove and opened the lid. A fine fragrance of caramel and chocolate rose from the tiny leaves that looked almost midnight blue as they curled in on themselves. The tin was nearly empty, and she knew deep inside that she'd been saving the last leaves to someday share with Geoffrey.

Her tea basket was still lost, but that didn't seem to matter now. People used to eat loose tea on long journeys. They'd pack it into hard little cakes they'd pull out later, to gnaw on while they warmed their hands by a fire. The tea provided physical sustenance, but it was also considered good for the soul.

Now Laura removed the kettle lid and poured the rest of the wedding tea into the cold water. She turned a white stove knob and a flame leaped to life.

"You're coming to tea with me, Geoffrey," she said aloud. "And I am going to read some Adrienne to you. It's my turn at the podium, but I promise not to lecture. You'll see."

In her mind, Geoffrey tried to turn and leave, but she caught his arm and led him to the dining room table.

"Sit down, Geoffrey. Please. I'll go get the Princeton."

Now she busied herself with bringing china, spoons, and napkins to the table. She set the white porcelain for Geoffrey and the roses teacup for herself. And she put Adrienne on her side of the table—*The Dream of a Common Language* now feeling like a promise that she and Geoffrey would, tonight, come to some kind of understanding.

Soon, the kettle began to whistle. Laura retrieved it, brought it to the table, and poured out its contents into their cups.

Geoffrey stared into his and began removing the floating leaves with his teaspoon. She put her hand on his and felt a surge of attraction. "Let it be. A few stray leaves won't hurt you. Consider it a new game you'll play with me."

She removed her hand from his warmth and sat down near her tea. Then Laura opened the book of poetry. She was ready to read. Geoffrey put his hand on the book and smoothly lowered it to the table. "No need for that, Laura. We've got words inside."

And again she felt a pang, a longing for what was, as he began to recite her old favorite, "Let me not to the marriage of true minds…"

Tears rose and she felt her throat closing up with a keen ache. She was not going to make it through this. She was not going to escape this warden of her mind.

Laura closed her eyes and began to give herself over to Geoffrey's words. She could feel herself losing strength with every line he spoke.

"Laura."

It was James.

"Laura, what are you going to write about in your novel?"

The question roused her as if from a dream.

"I'm not writing a novel, James."

"But you told me you wanted to write one."

"I do, James. Really, I do. But I'm not ready to start. And I'm not ready to finish by September. Megan is being unreasonable, and I don't know how to tell her that."

"Well, then," said James, "Why don't you just put that problem aside and start reading to Geoffrey? He's lost in his soliloquy and could use a good dose of Adrienne right now."

Laura nodded to James and wiped the tears from her eyes.

"Stop it, Geoffrey," she said. "It's my turn, remember? And it's okay. You gave Adrienne to me."

Geoffrey retracted his hand and sat in silence, while Laura began. She spoke with the resolve of a woman who'd been struck by lightning and lived to tell the tale. She moved from poem to poem, reading snippets as if she was weaving threads into a narrative of her own. Leaning forward, she shared...

> "No one who survives to speak
> new language, has avoided this:
> the cutting-away of an old force that held her
> rooted to an old ground
> the pitch of utter loneliness

I've been lonely, Geoffrey, for a long, long time. You know that, yes? I think you knew it from the beginning, that first night you asked me to your room and I let you speak some kind of solace onto my skin. Oh, listen to this, on page 76...

> Homesick for myself
> ...I am the lover and the loved,
> home and wanderer, she who splits
> firewood and she who knocks, a stranger
> in the storm

Do you think Mary Shelley was homesick for herself, Geoffrey? A self she'd been afraid to hold since birth? Could be, Geoffrey. Could be. Maybe that's why she wrote that huge novel. To find herself, or to etch herself onto some kind of landscape. Adrienne speaks of writing, Geoffrey. I love this part...

> I have written so many words
> wanting to live inside you
> to be of use to you

Now I must write for myself   for this blind
woman scratching the pavement with her wand of
   thought
this slippered crone   inching on icy sheets
reaching into wire trash baskets   pulling out
what was thrown away   and infinitely precious
I look at my hands and see... they are still unfinished
. . .

I look at my face in the glass   and see
a halfborn woman."

Laura raised her teacup and sipped the marriage tea. Geoffrey hadn't touched his, and she supposed that was his prerogative. She wasn't going to let his refusal dampen her own enthusiasm for the strong, fragrant brew.

"Adrienne says that when two women measure each other's spirits, eye to eye, a whole new poetry begins. I understand Adrienne's story, but do you suppose the two women could also be parts of one woman, like a person who looks into her reflection and speaks? Oh, anyway, the part that follows that bit about the two women is sort of longish, but it's worth listening to every word. Then we'll finish, Geoffrey, okay?

Vision begins to happen in such a life
as if a woman quietly walked away
from the argument and jargon in a room
and sitting down in the kitchen, began turning in her lap
bits of yarn, calico and velvet scraps,
laying them out absently on the scrubbed boards
in the lamplight, with small rainbow-colored shells..."

Laura lowered the book now and placed it on the table.

"It's alright, Geoffrey. You can go. I know you want to, and I want you to go. It's almost midnight, and I have a letter to write to someone before I go to sleep."

Geoffrey wiped his mouth with a napkin, though he hadn't actually eaten anything nor taken any tea. Then he stood and turned, and she watched the finality of his back to her, as he walked out of her imagination and into the night.

She carried his teacup to the kitchen and stood beside the sink. Hesitating for just a moment, she looked at the liquid that had filled the cup so beautifully. Then she overturned the porcelain.

30

It was Vargas Llosa who said that literary criticism, even when rigorous and inspired, could not entirely account for the process of creation. A successful fiction would always contain something inexplicable, something unbound. This was because, he noted, criticism is a form of reason that cannot, even with its finest net, capture certain factors crucial to a work—intuition, sensitivity, divination, or the elusive reality of chance.

In the end, he said nothing of the worm, but perhaps he didn't need to; after all, Vargas Llosa said that no one can teach anyone else to create and that his novice fiction writer, who'd spent so long in listening to his how-to tale, should simply forget everything he'd said in his letters and "just sit down and write."

To Laura, this supposed the possibility of what she had not wanted to admit: the worm. For you could not share such an insatiable creature inside you with someone else. It was yours and yours alone.

She cleared the teaspoons, the napkins, and her roses teacup from the table, all the while thinking on Vargas Llosa. She must somehow communicate his sentiments to Megan.

A light breeze was coming in the kitchen window now, and she could hear a fresh round of rain pattering against leaves and glass, over flowers and perhaps upon the seaweed-shaped rosemary still flowing in her little garden.

When she wrote to Megan, she'd ask whether Megan liked to walk uncovered in the rain. She would tell her she planned to maybe write a novel about an old woman in a cottage, who set an extra plate and waited day after day for her daughter to come home.

But first, Laura needed to invite her own mother to tea. She would give her a bouquet of roses and a kiss that was unlike any she'd given in the past, though her mother would not know the difference.

Laura put her hand to the door and looked through the glass. Her laptop screen had gone dim and the Luna moth had landed on her keyboard.

Let it stay until morning, she thought. She would rise early to tell Megan *no*. And *yes*.

Thanks

For my sisters—you know who you are—who give me such bright hope, thank you. And for James Cummins, who lent his name to a fiction, so I could lie my way to someone's truth, if not my own.

Also from T. S. Poetry Press

Rumors of Water: Thoughts on Creativity & Writing, by L.L. Barkat

A few brave writers pull back the curtain to show us their creative process. Annie Dillard did this. So did Hemingway. Now L.L. Barkat has given us a thoroughly modern analysis of writing. Practical, yes, but also a gentle uncovering of the art of being a writer.

— Gordon Atkinson, author *Turtles All the Way Down*

Contingency Plans: Poems, by David K. Wheeler

Simultaneously eloquent and potently raw; intimate reflections on spirituality and maturation, in harmony and conflict, that reverberate through every human journey.

—Carol Cassella, author of National Bestseller *Oxygen*

Neruda's Memoirs: Poems, by Maureen E. Doallas

Maureen Doallas's poems delight us with the play of words and impress us with their struggle, to make sense of nature and our natures.

—A. Jay Adler, Professor of English at Los Angeles Southwest College

All T. S. Poetry Press titles are available online in e-book and print editions. Print editions also available through Ingram.

Follow T. S. Poetry Press on Facebook at
https://www.facebook.com/tspoetrypress

Made in the USA
Lexington, KY
31 October 2012